W.W. JACOBS – THE SHORT STORIES
VOLUME 6

William Wymark Jacobs was born on September 8th, 1863 in the Wapping district of London, England. Jacobs grew up near the docks, where his father was a wharf manager. The docks and river side would be a constant theme of his writing in years to come.

Although surrounded by poverty, he received a formal education in London, first at a private prep school and later at the Birkbeck Literary and Scientific Institute.

His working life began with a less than exciting clerical position at the Post Office Savings Bank. Jacobs put his imagination to good use writing short stories, sketches and articles, many for the Post Office house publication "Blackfriars Magazine."

In 1896 Jacobs published Many Cargoes, a selection of sea-faring yarns, which established him as a popular writer with a knack for authentic dialogue and trick endings.

A year later he published a novelette, The Skipper's Wooing, and in 1898 another collection of short stories; Sea Urchins. These works painted vivid pictures of dockland and seafaring London full of colourful characters.

By 1899, Jacobs was able to quit the post office and write full-time.

He married the noted suffragist Agnes Eleanor Williams (who had been jailed for her protest activities) in 1900. They set up households both in Loughton, Essex and in central London.

The publication in 1902 of At Sunwich Port and Dialstone Lane, in 1904, cemented Jacobs' reputation as one of the leading British authors of the new century.

There followed a string of further successful publications, including Captain's All (1905), Night Watches (1914), The Castaways (1916), and Sea Whispers (1926).

Though Jacobs would create little in the way of new work after 1911, he still wrote and was recognized as a leading humorist, ranked alongside such writers as P. G. Wodehouse.

William Wymark Jacobs died in a North London nursing home in Hornsey Lane, Islington on September 1st, 1943.

Index of Contents

FRIENDS IN NEED

R. Joseph Gibbs finished his half-pint in the private bar of the Red Lion with the slowness of a man unable to see where the next was coming from, and, placing the mug on the counter, filled his pipe from a small paper of tobacco and shook his head slowly at his companions.

"First I've 'ad since ten o'clock this morning," he said, in a hard voice.

"Cheer up," said Mr. George Brown.

"It can't go on for ever," said Bob Kidd, encouragingly.

"All I ask for—is work," said Mr. Gibbs, impressively. "Not slavery, mind yer, but work."

"It's rather difficult to distinguish," said Mr. Brown.

"'Specially for some people," added Mr. Kidd.

"Go on," said Mr. Gibbs, gloomily. "Go on. Stand a man 'arf a pint, and then go and hurt 'is feelings. Twice yesterday I wondered to myself what it would feel like to make a hole in the water."

"Lots o' chaps do do it," said Mr. Brown, musingly.

"And leave their wives and families to starve," said Mr. Gibbs, icily.

"Very often the wife is better off," said his friend. "It's one mouth less for her to feed. Besides, she gen'rally gets something. When pore old Bill went they 'ad a Friendly Lead at the 'King's Head' and got his missis pretty nearly seventeen pounds."

"And I believe we'd get more than that for your old woman," said Mr. Kidd. "There's no kids, and she could keep 'erself easy. Not that I want to encourage you to make away with yourself."

Mr. Gibbs scowled and, tilting his mug, peered gloomily into the interior.

"Joe won't make no 'ole in the water," said Mr. Brown, wagging his head. "If it was beer, now—"

Mr. Gibbs turned and, drawing himself up to five feet three, surveyed the speaker with an offensive stare.

"I don't see why he need make a 'ole in anything," said Mr. Kidd, slowly. "It 'ud do just as well if we said he 'ad. Then we could pass the hat round and share it."

"Divide it into three halves and each 'ave one," said Mr. Brown, nodding; "but 'ow is it to be done?"

"'Ave some more beer and think it over," said Mr. Kidd, pale with excitement. "Three pints, please."

He and Mr. Brown took up their pints, and nodded at each other. Mr. Gibbs, toying idly with the handle of his, eyed them carefully. "Mind, I'm not promising anything," he said, slowly. "Understand, I ain't a-committing of myself by drinking this 'ere pint."

"You leave it to me, Joe," said Mr. Kidd.

Mr. Gibbs left it to him after a discussion in which pints played a persuasive part; with the result that Mr. Brown, sitting in the same bar the next evening with two or three friends, was rudely disturbed by the cyclonic entrance of Mr. Kidd, who, dripping with water, sank on a bench and breathed heavily.

"What's up? What's the matter?" demanded several voices.

"It's Joe—poor Joe Gibbs," said Mr. Kidd. "I was on Smith's wharf shifting that lighter to the next berth, and, o' course Joe must come aboard to help. He was shoving her off with 'is foot when—"

He broke off and shuddered and, accepting a mug of beer, pending the arrival of some brandy that a sympathizer had ordered, drank it slowly.

"It all 'appened in a flash," he said, looking round. "By the time I 'ad run round to his end he was just going down for the third time. I hung over the side and grabbed at 'im, and his collar and tie came off in my hand. Nearly went in, I did."

He held out the collar and tie; and approving notice was taken of the fact that he was soaking wet from the top of his head to the middle button of his waistcoat.

"Pore chap!" said the landlord, leaning over the bar. "He was in 'ere only 'arf an hour ago, standing in this very bar."

"Well, he's 'ad his last drop o' beer," said a carman in a chastened voice.

"That's more than anybody can say," said the landlord, sharply. "I never heard anything against the man; he's led a good life so far as I know, and 'ow can we tell that he won't 'ave beer?"

He made Mr. Kidd a present of another small glass of brandy.

"He didn't leave any family, did he?" he inquired, as he passed it over.

"Only a wife," said Mr. Kidd; "and who's to tell that pore soul I don't know. She fair doated on 'im. 'Ow she's to live I don't know. I shall do what I can for 'er."

"Same 'ere," said Mr. Brown, in a deep voice.

"Something ought to be done for 'er," said the carman, as he went out.

"First thing is to tell the police," said the landlord. "They ought to know; then p'r'aps one of them'll tell her. It's what they're paid for."

"It's so awfully sudden. I don't know where I am 'ardly," said Mr. Kidd. "I don't believe she's got a penny-piece in the 'ouse. Pore Joe 'ad a lot o' pals. I wonder whether we could'nt get up something for her."

"Go round and tell the police first," said the landlord, pursing up his lips thoughtfully. "We can talk about that later on."

Mr. Kidd thanked him warmly and withdrew, accompanied by Mr. Brown. Twenty minutes later they left the station, considerably relieved at the matter-of-fact way in which the police had received the tidings, and, hurrying across London Bridge, made their way towards a small figure supporting its back against a post in the Borough market.

"Well?" said Mr. Gibbs, snappishly, as he turned at the sound of their footsteps.

"It'll be all right, Joe," said Mr. Kidd. "We've sowed the seed."

"Sowed the wot?" demanded the other.

Mr. Kidd explained.

"Ho!" said Mr. Gibbs. "An' while your precious seed is a-coming up, wot am I to do? Wot about my comfortable 'ome? Wot about my bed and grub?"

His two friends looked at each other uneasily. In the excitement of the arrangements they had for gotten these things, and a long and sometimes painful experience of Mr. Gibbs showed them only too plainly where they were drifting.

"You'll 'ave to get a bed this side o' the river somewhere," said Mr. Brown, slowly. "Coffee-shop or something; and a smart, active man wot keeps his eyes open can always pick up a little money."

Mr. Gibbs laughed.

"And mind," said Mr. Kidd, furiously, in reply to the laugh, "anything we lend you is to be paid back out of your half when you get it. And, wot's more, you don't get a ha'penny till you've come into a barber's shop and 'ad them whiskers off. We don't want no accidents."

Mr. Gibbs, with his back against the post, fought for his whiskers for nearly half an hour, and at the end of that time was led into a barber's, and in a state of sullen indignation proffered his request for a "clean" shave. He gazed at the bare-faced creature that confronted him in the glass after the operation in open-eyed consternation, and Messrs. Kidd and Brown's politeness easily gave way before their astonishment.

"Well, I may as well have a 'air-cut while I'm here," said Mr. Gibbs, after a lengthy survey.

"And a shampoo, sir?" said the assistant.

"Just as you like," said Mr. Gibbs, turning a deaf ear to the frenzied expostulations of his financial backers. "Wot is it?"

He sat in amazed discomfort during the operation, and emerging with his friends remarked that he felt half a stone lighter. The information was received in stony silence, and, having spent some time in the selection, they found a quiet public-house, and in a retired corner formed themselves into a Committee of Ways and Means.

"That'll do for you to go on with," said Mr. Kidd, after he and Mr. Brown had each made a contribution; "and, mind, it's coming off of your share."

Mr. Gibbs nodded. "And any evening you want to see me you'll find me in here," he remarked. "Beer's ripping. Now you'd better go and see my old woman."

The two friends departed, and, to their great relief, found a little knot of people outside the abode of Mrs. Gibbs. It was clear that the news had been already broken, and, pushing their way upstairs, they found the widow with a damp handkerchief in her hand surrounded by attentive friends. In feeble accents she thanked Mr. Kidd for his noble attempts at rescue.

"He ain't dry yet," said Mr. Brown.

"I done wot I could," said Mr. Kidd, simply. "Pore Joe! Nobody could ha' had a better pal. Nobody!"

"Always ready to lend a helping 'and to them as was in trouble, he was," said Mr. Brown, looking round.

"'Ear, 'ear!" said a voice.

"And we'll lend 'im a helping 'and," said Mr. Kidd, energetically. "We can't do 'im no good, pore chap, but we can try and do something for 'er as is left behind."

He moved slowly to the door, accompanied by Mr. Brown, and catching the eye of one or two of the men beckoned them to follow. Under his able guidance a small but gradually increasing crowd made its way to the "Red Lion." For the next three or four days the friends worked unceasingly. Cards stating that a Friendly Lead would be held at the "Red Lion," for the benefit of the widow of the late Mr. Joseph Gibbs, were distributed broadcast; and anecdotes portraying a singularly rare and beautiful character obtained an even wider circulation. Too late Wapping realized the benevolent disposition and the kindly but unobtrusive nature that had departed from it for ever.

Mr. Gibbs, from his retreat across the water, fully shared his friends' enthusiasm, but an insane desire—engendered by vanity—to be present at the function was a source of considerable trouble and annoyance to them. When he offered to black his face and take part in the entertainment as a nigger minstrel, Mr. Kidd had to be led outside and kept there until such time as he could converse in English pure and undefiled.

"Getting above 'imself, that's wot it is," said Mr. Brown, as they wended their way home. "He's having too much money out of us to spend; but it won't be for long now."

"He's having a lord's life of it, while we're slaving ourselves to death," grumbled Mr. Kidd. "I never see 'im looking so fat and well. By rights he oughtn't to 'ave the same share as wot we're going to 'ave; he ain't doing none of the work."

His ill-humour lasted until the night of the "Lead," which, largely owing to the presence of a sporting fishmonger who had done well at the races that day, and some of his friends, realized a sum far beyond the expectations of the hard-working promoters. The fishmonger led off by placing a five-pound note in the plate, and the packed audience breathed so hard that the plate-holder's responsibility began to weigh upon his spirits. In all, a financial tribute of thirty-seven pounds three and fourpence was paid to the memory of the late Mr. Gibbs.

"Over twelve quid apiece," said the delighted Mr. Kidd as he bade his co-worker good night. "Sounds too good to be true."

The next day passed all too slowly, but work was over at last, and Mr. Kidd led the way over London Bridge a yard or two ahead of the more phlegmatic Mr. Brown. Mr. Gibbs was in his old corner at the "Wheelwright's Arms," and, instead of going into ecstasies over the sum realized, hinted darkly that it would have been larger if he had been allowed to have had a hand in it.

"It'll 'ardly pay me for my trouble," he said, shaking his head. "It's very dull over 'ere all alone by myself. By the time you two have 'ad your share, besides taking wot I owe you, there'll be 'ardly anything left."

"I'll talk to you another time," said Mr. Kidd, regarding him fixedly. "Wot you've got to do now is to come acrost the river with us."

"What for?" demanded Mr. Gibbs.

"We're going to break the joyful news to your old woman that you're alive afore she starts spending money wot isn't hers," said Mr. Kidd. "And we want you to be close by in case she don't believe us.

"Well, do it gentle, mind," said the fond husband. "We don't want 'er screaming, or anything o' that sort. I know 'er better than wot you do, and my advice to you is to go easy."

He walked along by the side of them, and, after some demur, consented, as a further disguise, to put on a pair of spectacles, for which Mr. Kidd's wife's mother had been hunting high and low since eight o'clock that morning.

"You doddle about 'ere for ten minutes," said Mr. Kidd, as they reached the Monument, "and then foller on. When you pass a lamp-post 'old your handkerchief up to your face. And wait for us at the corner of your road till we come for you."

He went off at a brisk pace with Mr. Brown, a pace moderated to one of almost funeral solemnity as they approached the residence of Mrs. Gibbs. To their relief she was alone, and after the usual amenities thanked them warmly for all they had done for her.

"I'd do more than that for pore Joe," said Mr. Brown.

"They—they 'aven't found 'im yet?" said the widow.

Mr. Kidd shook his head. "My idea is they won't find 'im," he said, slowly.

"Went down on the ebb tide," explained Mr. Brown; and spoilt Mr. Kidd's opening.

"Wherever he is 'e's better off," said Mrs. Gibbs.

"No more trouble about being out o' work; no more worry; no more pain. We've all got to go some day.

"Yes," began Mr. Kidd; "but—

"I'm sure I don't wish 'im back," said Mrs. Gibbs; "that would be sinful."

"But 'ow if he wanted to come back?" said Mr. Kidd, playing for an opening.

"And 'elp you spend that money," said Mr. Brown, ignoring the scowls of his friend.

Mrs. Gibbs looked bewildered. "Spend the money?" she began.

"Suppose," said Mr. Kidd, "suppose he wasn't drownded after all? Only last night I dreamt he was alive."

"So did I," said Mr. Brown.

"He was smiling at me," said Mr. Kidd, in a tender voice. "'Bob,' he ses, 'go and tell my pore missis that I'm alive,' he ses; 'break it to 'er gentle.'"

"It's the very words he said to me in my dream," said Mr. Brown. "Bit strange, ain't it?"

"Very," said Mrs. Gibbs.

"I suppose," said Mr. Kidd, after a pause, "I suppose you haven't been dreaming about 'im?"

"No; I'm a teetotaller," said the widow.

The two gentlemen exchanged glances, and Mr. Kidd, ever of an impulsive nature, resolved to bring matters to a head.

"Wot would you do if Joe was to come in 'ere at this door?" he asked.

"Scream the house down," said the widow, promptly.

"Scream—scream the 'ouse down?" said the distressed Mr. Kidd.

Mrs. Gibbs nodded. "I should go screaming, raving mad," she said, with conviction.

"But—but not if 'e was alive!" said Mr. Kidd.

"I don't know what you're driving at," said Mrs. Gibbs. "Why don't you speak out plain? Poor Joe is drownded, you know that; you saw it all, and yet you come talking to me about dreams and things."

Mr. Kidd bent over her and put his hand affectionately on her shoulder. "He escaped," he said, in a thrilling whisper. "He's alive and well."

"WHAT?" said Mrs. Gibbs, starting back.

"True as I stand 'ere," said Mr. Kidd; "ain't it, George?"

"Truer," said Mr. Brown, loyally.

Mrs. Gibbs leaned back, gasping. "Alive!" she said. "But 'ow? 'Ow can he be?"

"Don't make such a noise," said Mr. Kidd, earnestly. "Mind, if anybody else gets to 'ear of it you'll 'ave to give that money back."

"I'd give more than that to get 'im back," said Mrs. Gibbs, wildly. "I believe you're deceiving me."

"True as I stand 'ere," asseverated the other. "He's only a minute or two off, and if it wasn't for you screaming I'd go out and fetch 'im in."

"I won't scream," said Mrs. Gibbs, "not if I know it's flesh and blood. Oh, where is he? Why don't you bring 'im in? Let me go to 'im."

"All right," said Mr. Kidd, with a satisfied smile at Mr. Brown; "all in good time. I'll go and fetch 'im now; but, mind, if you scream you'll spoil everything."

He bustled cheerfully out of the room and downstairs, and Mrs. Gibbs, motioning Mr. Brown to silence, stood by the door with parted lips, waiting. Three or four minutes elapsed.

"'Ere they come," said Mr. Brown, as footsteps sounded on the stairs. "Now, no screaming, mind!"

Mrs. Gibbs drew back, and, to the gratification of all concerned, did not utter a sound as Mr. Kidd, followed by her husband, entered the room. She stood looking expectantly towards the doorway.

"Where is he?" she gasped.

"Eh?" said Mr. Kidd, in a startled voice. "Why here. Don't you know 'im?"

"It's me, Susan," said Mr. Gibbs, in a low voice.

"Oh, I might 'ave known it was a joke," cried Mrs. Gibbs, in a faint voice, as she tottered to a chair. "Oh,'ow cruel of you to tell me my pore Joe was alive! Oh, 'ow could you?"

"Lor' lumme," said the incensed Mr. Kidd, pushing Mr. Gibbs forward. "Here he is. Same as you saw 'im last, except for 'is whiskers. Don't make that sobbing noise; people'll be coming in."

"Oh! Oh! Oh! Take 'im away," cried Mrs. Gibbs. "Go and play your tricks with somebody else's broken 'art."

"But it's your husband," said Mr. Brown.

"Take 'im away," wailed Mrs. Gibbs.

Mr. Kidd, grinding his teeth, tried to think. "'Ave you got any marks on your body, Joe?" he inquired.

"I ain't got a mark on me," said Mr. Gibbs with a satisfied air, "or a blemish. My skin is as whi—"

"That's enough about your skin," interrupted Mr. Kidd, rudely.

"If you ain't all of you gone before I count ten," said Mrs. Gibbs, in a suppressed voice, "I'll scream. 'Ow dare you come into a respectable woman's place and talk about your skins? Are you going? One! Two! Three! Four! Five!"

Her voice rose with each numeral; and Mr. Gibbs himself led the way downstairs, and, followed by his friends, slipped nimbly round the corner.

"It's a wonder she didn't rouse the whole 'ouse," he said, wiping his brow on his sleeve; "and where should we ha' been then? I thought at the time it was a mistake you making me 'ave my whiskers off, but I let you know best. She's never seen me without 'em. I 'ad a remarkable strong growth when I was quite a boy. While other boys was—"

"Shut-up!" vociferated Mr. Kidd.

"Sha'n't!" said Mr. Gibbs, defiantly. "I've 'ad enough of being away from my comfortable little 'ome and my wife; and I'm going to let 'em start growing agin this very night. She'll never reckernize me without 'em, that's certain."

"He's right, Bob," said Mr. Brown, with conviction.

"D'ye mean to tell me we've got to wait till 'is blasted whiskers grow?" cried Mr. Kidd, almost dancing with fury. "And go on keeping 'im in idleness till they do?"

"You'll get it all back out o' my share," said Mr. Gibbs, with dignity. "But you can please yourself. If you like to call it quits now, I don't mind."

Mr. Brown took his seething friend aside, and conferred with him in low but earnest tones. Mr. Gibbs, with an indifferent air, stood by whistling softly.

"'Ow long will they take to grow?" inquired Mr. Kidd, turning to him with a growl.

Mr. Gibbs shrugged his shoulders. "Can't say," he replied; "but I should think two or three weeks would be enough for 'er to reckernize me by. If she don't, we must wait another week or so, that's all."

"Well, there won't be much o' your share left, mind that," said Mr. Kidd, glowering at him.

"I can't help it," said Mr. Gibbs. "You needn't keep reminding me of it."

They walked the rest of the way in silence; and for the next fortnight Mr. Gibbs's friends paid nightly visits to note the change in his appearance, and grumble at its slowness.

"We'll try and pull it off to-morrow night," said Mr. Kidd, at the end of that period. "I'm fair sick o' lending you money."

Mr. Gibbs shook his head and spoke sagely about not spoiling the ship for a ha'porth o' tar; but Mr. Kidd was obdurate.

"There's enough for 'er to reckernize you by," he said, sternly, "and we don't want other people to. Meet us at the Monument at eight o'clock to-morrow night, and we'll get it over."

"Give your orders," said Mr. Gibbs, in a nasty voice.

"Keep your 'at well over your eyes," commanded Mr. Kidd, sternly. "Put them spectacles on wot I lent you, and it wouldn't be a bad idea if you tied your face up in a piece o' red flannel."

"I know wot I'm going to do without you telling me," said Mr. Gibbs, nodding. "I'll bet you pots round that you don't either of you reckernize me tomorrow night."

The bet was taken at once, and from eight o'clock until ten minutes to nine the following night Messrs. Kidd and Brown did their best to win it. Then did Mr. Kidd, turning to Mr. Brown in perplexity, inquire with many redundant words what it all meant.

"He must 'ave gone on by 'imself," said Mr. Brown. "We'd better go and see."

In a state of some disorder they hurried back to Wapping, and, mounting the stairs to Mrs. Gibbs's room, found the door fast. To their fervent and repeated knocking there was no answer.

"Ah, you won't make her 'ear," said a woman, thrusting an untidy head over the balusters on the next landing. "She's gone."

"Gone!" exclaimed both gentlemen. "Where?"

"Canada," said the woman. "She went off this morning."

Mr. Kidd leaned up against the wall for support; Mr. Brown stood open-mouthed and voiceless.

"It was a surprise to me," said the woman, "but she told me this morning she's been getting ready on the quiet for the last fortnight. Good spirits she was in, too; laughing like anything."

"Laughing!" repeated Mr. Kidd, in a terrible voice.

The woman nodded. "And when I spoke about it and reminded 'er that she 'ad only just lost 'er pore husband, I thought she would ha' burst," she said, severely. "She sat down on that stair and laughed till the tears ran dowwn 'er face like water."

Mr. Brown turned a bewildered face upon his partner. "Laughing!" he said, slowly. "Wot 'ad she got to laugh at?"

"Two born-fools," replied Mr. Kidd.

GOOD INTENTIONS

"Jealousy; that's wot it is," said the night-watchman, trying to sneer—"pure jealousy." He had left his broom for a hurried half-pint at the "Bull's Head"—left it leaning in a negligent attitude against the warehouse-wall; now, lashed to the top of the crane at the jetty end, it pointed its soiled bristles towards the evening sky and defied capture.

"And I know who it is, and why 'e's done it," he continued. "Fust and last, I don't suppose I was talking to the gal for more than ten minutes, and 'arf of that was about the weather.

"I don't suppose anybody 'as suffered more from jealousy than wot I 'ave: Other people's jealousy, I mean. Ever since I was married the missis has been setting traps for me, and asking people to keep an eye on me. I blacked one of the eyes once—like a fool—and the chap it belonged to made up a tale about me that I ain't lived down yet.

"Years ago, when I was out with the missis one evening, I saved a gal's life for her. She slipped as she was getting off a bus, and I caught 'er just in time. Fine strapping gal she was, and afore I could get my balance we 'ad danced round and round 'arfway acrost the road with our arms round each other's necks, and my missis watching us from the pavement. When we were safe, she said the gal 'adn't slipped at all; and, as soon as the gal 'ad got 'er breath, I'm blest if she didn't say so too.

"You can't argufy with jealous people, and you can't shame 'em. When I told my missis once that I should never dream of being jealous of her, instead of up and thanking me for it, she spoilt the best frying-pan we ever had. When the widder-woman next-door but two and me 'ad rheumatics at the same time, she went and asked the doctor whether it was catching.

"The worse trouble o' that kind I ever got into was all through trying to do somebody else a kindness. I went out o' my way to do it; I wasted the whole evening for the sake of other people, and got into such trouble over it that even now it gives me the cold shivers to think of.

"Cap'n Tarbell was the man I tried to do a good turn to; a man what used to be master of a ketch called the *Lizzie and Annie,* trading between 'ere and Shoremouth. 'Artful Jack' he used to be called, and if ever a man deserved the name, he did. A widder-man of about fifty, and as silly as a boy of fifteen. He 'ad been talking of getting married agin for over ten years, and, thinking it was only talk, I didn't give 'im any good advice. Then he told me one night that 'e was keeping company with a woman named Lamb, who lived at a place near Shoremouth. When I asked 'im what she looked like, he said that she had a good 'art, and, knowing wot that meant, I wasn't at all surprised when he told me some time arter that 'e had been a silly fool.

"'Well, if she's got a good 'art,' I ses, 'p'r'aps she'll let you go.'

"'Talk sense,' he ses. 'It ain't good enough for that. Why, she worships the ground I tread on. She thinks there is nobody like me in the whole wide world.'

"'Let's 'ope she'll think so arter you're married,' I ses, trying to cheer him up.

"'I'm not going to get married,' he ses. 'Leastways, not to 'er. But 'ow to get out of it without breaking her 'art and being had up for breach o' promise I can't think. And if the other one got to 'ear of it, I should lose her too.'

"'Other one?' I ses, 'wot other one?'

"Cap'n Tarbell shook his 'ead and smiled like a silly gal.

"'She fell in love with me on top of a bus in the Mile End Road,' he ses. 'Love at fust sight it was. She's a widder lady with a nice little 'ouse at Bow, and plenty to live on-her 'usband having been a builder. I don't know what to do. You see, if I married both of 'em it's sure to be found out sooner or later.'

"'You'll be found out as it is,' I ses, 'if you ain't careful. I'm surprised at you.'

"'Yes,' he ses, getting up and walking backwards and forwards; 'especially as Mrs. Plimmer is always talking about coming down to see the ship. One thing is, the crew won't give me away; they've been with me too long for that. P'r'aps you could give me a little advice, Bill.'

"I did. I talked to that man for an hour and a'arf, and when I 'ad finished he said he didn't want that kind of advice at all. Wot 'e wanted was for me to tell 'im 'ow to get rid of Miss Lamb and marry Mrs. Plimmer without anybody being offended or having their feelings hurt.

"Mrs. Plimmer came down to the ship the very next evening. Fine-looking woman she was, and, wot with 'er watch and chain and di'mond rings and brooches and such-like, I should think she must 'ave 'ad five or six pounds' worth of jewell'ry on 'er. She gave me a very pleasant smile, and I gave 'er one back, and we stood chatting there like old friends till at last she tore 'erself away and went on board the ship.

"She came off by and by hanging on Cap'n Tarbell's arm. The cap'n was dressed up in 'is Sunday clothes, with one of the cleanest collars on I 'ave ever seen in my life, and smoking a cigar that smelt like an escape of gas. He came back alone at ha'past eleven that night, and 'e told me that if it wasn't for the other one down Shoremouth way he should be the 'appiest man on earth.

"'Mrs. Plimmer's only got one fault,' he ses, shaking his 'cad, 'and that's jealousy. If she got to know of Laura Lamb, it would be all U.P. It makes me go cold all over when I think of it. The only thing is to get married as quick as I can; then she can't help 'erself.'

"'It wouldn't prevent the other one making a fuss, though,' I ses.

"'No,' he ses, very thoughtfully, 'it wouldn't. I shall 'ave to do something there, but wot, I don't know.'

"He climbed on board like a man with a load on his mind, and arter a look at the sky went below and forgot both 'is troubles in sleep.

"Mrs. Plimmer came down to the wharf every time the ship was up, arter that. Sometimes she'd spend the evening aboard, and sometimes they'd go off and spend it somewhere else. She 'ad a fancy for the cabin, I think, and the cap'n told me that she 'ad said when they were married she was going to sail with 'im sometimes.

"'But it ain't for six months yet,' he ses, 'and a lot o' things might 'appen to the other one in that time, with luck.'

"It was just about a month arter that that 'e came to me one evening trembling all over. I 'ad just come on dooty, and afore I could ask 'im wot was the matter he 'ad got me in the 'Bull's Head' and stood me three 'arf-pints, one arter the other.

"'I'm ruined,' he ses in a 'usky whisper; 'I'm done for. Why was wimmen made? Wot good are they? Fancy 'ow bright and 'appy we should all be without 'em.'

"'I started to p'int out one or two things to 'im that he seemed to 'ave forgot, but 'e wouldn't listen. He was so excited that he didn't seem to know wot 'e was doing, and arter he 'ad got three more 'arf-pints waiting for me, all in a row on the counter, I 'ad to ask 'im whether he thought I was there to do conjuring tricks, or wot?'

"'There was a letter waiting for me in the office,' he ses. 'From Miss Lamb—she's in London. She's coming to pay me a surprise visit this evening—I know who'll get the surprise. Mrs. Plimmer's coming too.'

"I gave 'im one of my 'arf-pints and made 'im drink it. He chucked the pot on the floor when he 'ad done, in a desprit sort o' way, and 'im and the landlord 'ad a little breeze then that did 'im more good than wot the beer 'ad. When we came outside 'e seemed more contented with 'imself, but he shook his 'ead and got miserable as soon as we got to the wharf agin.

"'S'pose they both come along at the same time,' he ses. 'Wot's to be done?'

"I shut the gate with a bang and fastened the wicket. Then I turned to 'im with a smile.

"'I'm watchman 'ere,' I ses, 'and I lets in who I thinks I will. This ain't a public 'ighway,' I ses; 'it's a wharf.'

"'Bill,' he ses, 'you're a genius.'

"'If Miss Lamb comes 'ere asking arter you,' I ses, 'I shall say you've gone out for the evening.'

"'Wot about her letter?' he ses.

"'You didn't 'ave it,' I ses, winking at 'im.

"'And suppose she waits about outside for me, and Mrs. Plimmer wants me to take 'er out?' he ses, shivering. 'She's a fearful obstinate woman; and she'd wait a week for me.'

"He kept peeping up the road while we talked it over, and then we both see Mrs. Plimmer coming along. He backed on to the wharf and pulled out 'is purse.

"'Bill,' he ses, gabbling as fast as 'e could gabble, 'here's five or six shillings. If the other one comes and won't go away tell 'er I've gone to the Pagoda Music-'all and you'll take 'er to me, keep 'er out all the evening some'ow, if you can, if she comes back too soon keep 'er in the office.'

"'And wot about leaving the wharf and my dooty?' I ses, staring.

"'I'll put Joe on to keep watch for you,' he ses, pressing the money in my 'and. 'I rely on you, Bill, and I'll never forget you. You won't lose by it, trust me.'

"He nipped off and tumbled aboard the ship afore I could say a word. I just stood there staring arter 'im and feeling the money, and afore I could make up my mind Mrs. Plimmer came up.

"I thought I should never ha' got rid of 'er. She stood there chatting and smiling, and seemed to forget all about the cap'n, and every moment I was afraid that the other one might come up. At last she went off, looking behind 'er, to the ship, and then I went outside and put my back up agin the gate and waited.

"I 'ad hardly been there ten minutes afore the other one came along. I saw 'er stop and speak to a policeman, and then she came straight over to me.

"'I want to see Cap'n Tarbell,' she ses.

"'Cap'n Tarbell?' I ses, very slow; 'Cap'n Tarbell 'as gone off for the evening.'

"'Gone off!' she ses, staring. 'But he can't 'ave. Are you sure?'

"'Sartain,' I ses. Then I 'ad a bright idea. 'And there's a letter come for 'im,' I ses.

"'Oh, dear!' she ses. 'And I thought it would be in plenty of time. Well, I must go on the ship and wait for 'im, I suppose.'

"If I 'ad only let 'er go I should ha' saved myself a lot o' trouble, and the man wot deserved it would ha' got it. Instead o' that I told 'er about the music-'all, and arter carrying on like a silly gal o' seventeen and saying she couldn't think of it, she gave way and said she'd go with me to find 'im. I was all right so far as clothes went as it happened. Mrs. Plimmer said once that I got more and more dressy every time she saw me, and my missis 'ad said the same thing only in a different way. I just took a peep through the wicket and saw that Joe 'ad taken up my dooty, and then we set off.

"I said I wasn't quite sure which one he'd gone to, but we'd try the Pagoda Music-'all fust, and we went there on a bus from Aldgate. It was the fust evening out I 'ad 'ad for years, and I should 'ave enjoyed it if it 'adn't been for Miss Lamb. Wotever Cap'n Tarbell could ha' seen in 'er, I can't think.

"She was quiet, and stupid, and bad-tempered. When the bus-conductor came round for the fares she 'adn't got any change; and when we got to the hall she did such eggsterrordinary things trying to find 'er pocket that I tried to look as if she didn't belong to me. When she left off she smiled and said she was farther off than ever, and arter three or four wot was standing there 'ad begged 'er to have another try, I 'ad to pay for the two.

"The 'ouse was pretty full when we got in, but she didn't take no notice of that. Her idea was that she could walk about all over the place looking for Cap'n Tarbell, and it took three men in buttons and a policeman to persuade 'er different. We were pushed into a couple o' seats at last, and then she started finding fault with me.

"'Where is Cap'n Tarbell?' she ses. 'Why don't you find him?'

"'I'll go and look for 'im in the bar presently,' I ses. 'He's sure to be there, arter a turn or two.'

"I managed to keep 'er quiet for 'arf an hour—with the 'elp of the people wot sat near us—and then I 'ad to go. I 'ad a glass o' beer to pass the time away, and, while I was drinking it, who should come up but the cook and one of the hands from the *Lizzie and Annie*.

"'We saw you,' ses the cook, winking; 'didn't we Bob?'

"'Yes,' ses Bob, shaking his silly 'ead; 'but it wasn't no surprise to me. I've 'ad my eye on 'im for a long time past.'

"'I thought 'e was married,' ses the cook.

"'So he is,' ses Bob, 'and to the best wife in London. I know where she lives. Mine's a bottle o' Bass,' he ses, turning to me.

"'So's mine,' ses the cook.

"I paid for two bottles for 'em, and arter that they said that they'd 'ave a whisky and soda apiece just to show as there was no ill-feeling.

"'It's very good,' ses Bob, sipping his, 'but it wants a sixpenny cigar to go with it. It's been the dream o' my life to smoke a sixpenny cigar.'

"'So it 'as mine,' ses the cook, 'but I don't suppose I ever shall.'

"They both coughed arter that, and like a goodnatured fool I stood 'em a sixpenny cigar apiece, and I 'ad just turned to go back to my seat when up come two more hands from the Lizzie and Annie.

"'Halloa, watchman!' ses one of 'em. 'Why, I thought you was a-taking care of the wharf.'

"'He's got something better than the wharf to take care of,' ses Bob, grinning.

"'I know; we see 'im,' ses the other chap. 'We've been watching 'is goings-on for the last 'arf-hour; better than a play it was.'

"I stopped their mouths with a glass o' bitter each, and went back to my seat while they was drinking it. I told Miss Lamb in whispers that 'e wasn't there, but I'd 'ave another look for him by and by. If she'd ha' whispered back it would ha' been all right, but she wouldn't, and, arter a most unpleasant scene, she walked out with her 'ead in the air follered by me with two men in buttons and a policeman.

"O' course, nothing would do but she must go back to the wharf and wait for Cap'n Tarbell, and all the way there I was wondering wot would 'appen if she went on board and found 'im there with Mrs. Plimmer. However, when we got there I persuaded 'er to go into the office while I went aboard to see if I could find out where he was, and three minutes arterwards he was standing with me behind the galley, trembling all over and patting me on the back.

"'Keep 'er in the office a little longer,' he ses, in a whisper. 'The other's going soon. Keep 'er there as long as you can.'

"'And suppose she sees you and Mrs. Plimmer passing the window?' I ses.

"'That'll be all right; I'm going to take 'er to the stairs in the ship's boat,' he ses. 'It's more romantic.'

"He gave me a little punch in the ribs, playfullike, and, arter telling me I was worth my weight in gold-dust, went back to the cabin agin.

"I told Miss Lamb that the cabin was locked up, but that Cap'n Tarbell was expected back in about 'arf-an-hour's time. Then I found 'er an old newspaper and a comfortable chair and sat down to wait. I couldn't go on the wharf for fear she'd want to come with me, and I sat there as patient as I could, till a little clicking noise made us both start up and look at each other.

"'Wot's that?' she ses, listening.

"'It sounded,' I ses 'it sounded like somebody locking the door.'

"I went to the door to try it just as somebody dashed past the window with their 'ead down. It was locked fast, and arter I had 'ad a try at it and Miss Lamb had 'ad a try at it, we stood and looked at each other in surprise.

"'Somebody's playing a joke on us,' I ses.

"'Joke!' ses Miss Lamb. 'Open that door at once. If you don't open it I'll call for the police.'

"She looked at the windows, but the iron bars wot was strong enough to keep the vans outside was strong enough to keep 'er in, and then she gave way to such a fit o' temper that I couldn't do nothing with 'er.

"'Cap'n Tarbell can't be long now,' I ses, as soon as I could get a word in. 'We shall get out as soon as e comes.'

"She flung 'erself down in the chair agin with 'er back to me, and for nearly three-quarters of an hour we sat there without a word. Then, to our joy, we 'eard footsteps turn in at the gate. Quick footsteps they was. Somebody turned the handle of the door, and then a face looked in at the window that made me nearly jump out of my boots in surprise. A face that was as white as chalk with temper, and a bonnet cocked over one eye with walking fast. She shook 'er fist at me, and then she shook it at Miss Lamb.

"'Who's that?' ses Miss Lamb.

"'My missis,' I ses, in a loud voice. 'Thank goodness she's come.'

"'Open the door!' ses my missis, with a screech.

"'OPEN THE DOOR!'

"'I can't,' I ses. 'Somebody's locked it. This is Cap'n Tarbell's young lady.'

"'I'll Cap'n Tarbell 'er when I get in!' ses my wife. 'You too. I'll music-'all you! I'll learn you to go gallivanting about! Open the door!'

"She walked up and down the alley-way in front of the window waiting for me just like a lion walking up and down its cage waiting for its dinner, and I made up my mind then and there that I should 'ave to make a clean breast of it and let Cap'n Tarbell get out of it the best way he could. I wasn't going to suffer for him.

"'Ow long my missis walked up and down there I don't know. It seemed ages to me; but at last I 'eard footsteps and voices, and Bob and the cook and the other two chaps wot we 'ad met at the music'all came along and stood grinning in at the window.

"'Somebody's locked us in,' I ses. 'Go and fetch Cap'n Tarbell.'

"'Cap'n Tarbell?' ses the cook. 'You don't want to see 'im. Why, he's the last man in the world you ought to want to see! You don't know 'ow jealous he is.'

"'You go and fetch 'im, I ses. "Ow dare you talk like that afore my wife!'

"'I dursen't take the responserbility,' ses the cook. 'It might mean bloodshed.'

"'You go and fetch 'im,' ses my missis. 'Never mind about the bloodshed. I don't. Open the door!'

"She started banging on the door agin, and arter talking among themselves for a time they moved off to the ship. They came back in three or four minutes, and the cook 'eld up something in front of the window.

"'The boy 'ad got it,' he ses. 'Now shall I open the door and let your missis in, or would you rather stay where you are in peace and quietness?'

"I saw my missis jump at the key, and Bob and the others, laughing fit to split their sides, 'olding her back. Then I heard a shout, and the next moment Cap'n Tarbell came up and asked 'em wot the trouble was about.

"They all started talking at once, and then the cap'n, arter one look in at the window, threw up his 'ands and staggered back as if 'e couldn't believe his eyesight. He stood dazed-like for a second or two, and then 'e took the key out of the cook's 'and, opened the door, and walked in. The four men was close be'ind 'im, and, do all she could, my missis couldn't get in front of 'em.

"'Watchman!' he ses, in a stuck-up voice, 'wot does this mean? Laura Lamb! wot 'ave you got to say for yourself? Where 'ave you been all the evening?'

"'She's been to a music-'all with Bill,' ses the cook. 'We saw 'em.'

"'WOT?' ses the cap'n, falling back again. 'It can't be!'

"'It was them,' ses my wife. 'A little boy brought me a note telling me. You let me go; it's my husband, and I want to talk to 'im.'

"'It's all right,' I ses, waving my 'and at Miss Lamb, wot was going to speak, and smiling at my missis, wot was trying to get at me.

"'We went to look for you,' ses Miss Lamb, very quick. 'He said you were at the music-'all, and as you 'adn't got my letter I thought it was very likely.'

"'But I did get your letter,' ses the cap'n.

"'He said you didn't,' ses Miss Lamb.

"'Look 'ere,' I ses. 'Why don't you keep quiet and let me explain? I can explain everything.'

"'I'm glad o' that, for your sake, my man,' ses the cap'n, looking at me very hard. 'I 'ope you will be able to explain 'ow it was you came to leave the wharf for three hours.'

"I saw it all then. If I split about Mrs. Plimmer, he'd split to the guv'nor about my leaving my dooty, and I should get the sack. I thought I should ha' choked, and, judging by the way they banged me on the back, Bob and the cook thought so too. They 'elped me to a chair when I got better, and I sat there 'elpless while the cap'n went on talking.

"'I'm no mischief-maker,' he ses; 'and, besides, p'r'aps he's been punished enough. And as far as I'm concerned he can take this lady to a music-'all every night of the week if 'e likes. I've done with her.'

"There was an eggsterrordinary noise from where my missis was standing; like the gurgling water makes sometimes running down the kitchen sink at 'ome, only worse. Then they all started talking together, and 'arf-a-dozen times or more Miss Lamb called me to back 'er up in wot she was saying, but I only shook my 'ead, and at last, arter tossing her 'ead at Cap'n Tarbell and telling 'im she wouldn't 'ave 'im if he'd got fifty million a year, the five of 'em 'eld my missis while she went off.

"They gave 'er ten minutes' start, and then Cap'n Tarbell, arter looking at me and shaking his 'ead, said he was afraid they must be going.

"'And I 'ope this night'll be a lesson to you,' he ses. 'Don't neglect your dooty again. I shall keep my eye on you, and if you be'ave yourself I sha'n't say anything. Why, for all you know or could ha' done the wharf might ha' been burnt to the ground while you was away!'

"He nodded to his crew, and they all walked out laughing and left me alone—with the missis."

THE GREY PARROT

The Chief Engineer and the Third sat at tea on the s.s. Curlew in the East India Docks. The small and not over-clean steward having placed everything he could think of upon the table, and then added everything the Chief could think of, had assiduously poured out two cups of tea and withdrawn by request. The two men ate steadily, conversing between bites, and interrupted occasionally by a hoarse and sepulchral voice, the owner of which, being much exercised by the sight of the food, asked for it, prettily at first, and afterwards in a way which at least compelled attention.

"That's pretty good for a parrot," said the Third critically. "Seems to know what he's saying too. No, don't give it anything. It'll stop if you do."

"There's no pleasure to me in listening to coarse language," said the Chief with dignity.

He absently dipped a piece of bread and butter in the Third's tea, and losing it chased it round and round the bottom of the cap with his finger, the Third regarding the operation with an interest and emotion which he was at first unable to understand.

"You'd better pour yourself out another cup," he said thoughtfully as he caught the Third's eye.

"I'm going to," said the other dryly.

"The man I bought it off," said the Chief, giving the bird the sop, "said that it was a perfectly respectable parrot and wouldn't know a bad word if it heard it I hardly like to give it to my wife now."

"It's no good being too particular," said the Third, regarding him with an ill-concealed grin; "that's the worst of all you young married fellows. Seem to think your wife has got to be wrapped up in brown paper. Ten chances to one she'll be amused."

The Chief shrugged his shoulders disdainfully. "I bought the bird to be company for her," he said slowly; "she'll be very lonesome without me, Rogers."

"How do you know?" inquired the other.

"She said so," was the reply.

"When you've been married as long as I have," said the Third, who having been married some fifteen years felt that their usual positions were somewhat reversed, "you'll know that generally speaking they're glad to get rid of you."

"What for?" demanded the Chief in a voice that Othello might have envied.

"Well, you get in the way a bit," said Rogers with secret enjoyment; "you see you upset the arrangements. House-cleaning and all that sort of thing gets interrupted. They're glad to see you back at first, and then glad to see the back of you."

"There's wives and wives," said the bridegroom tenderly.

"And mine's a good one," said the Third, "registered A1 at Lloyd's, but she don't worry about me going away. Your wife's thirty years younger than you, isn't she?"

"Twenty-five," corrected the other shortly. "You see what I'm afraid of is, that she'll get too much attention."

"Well, women like that," remarked the Third.

"But I don't, damn it," cried the Chief hotly. "When I think of it I get hot all over. Boiling hot."

"That won't last," said the other reassuringly; "you won't care twopence this time next year."

"We're not all alike," growled the Chief; "some of us have got finer feelings than others have. I saw the chap next door looking at her as we passed him this morning."

"Lor'," said the Third.

"I don't want any of your damned impudence," said the Chief sharply. "He put his hat on straighter when he passed us. What do you think of that?"

"Can't say," replied the other with commendable gravity; "it might mean anything."

"If he has any of his nonsense while I'm away I'll break his neck," said the Chief passionately. "I shall know of it."

The other raised his eyebrows.

"I've asked the landlady to keep her eyes open a bit," said the Chief. "My wife was brought up in the country, and she's very young and simple, so that it is quite right and proper for her to have a motherly old body to look after her."

"Told your wife?" queried Rogers.

"No," said the other. "Fact is, I've got an idea about that parrot. I'm going to tell her it's a magic bird, and will tell me everything she does while I'm away. Anything the landlady tells me I shall tell her I got from the parrot. For one thing, I don't want her to go out after seven of an evening, and she's promised me she won't. If she does I shall know, and pretend that I know through the parrot What do you think of it?"

"Think of it?" said the Third, staring at him. "Think of it? Fancy a man telling a grown-up woman a yarn like that!"

"She believes in warnings and death-watches, and all that sort of thing," said the Chief, "so why shouldn't she?"

"Well, you'll know whether she believes in it or not when you come back," said Rogers, "and it'll be a great pity, because it's a beautiful talker."

"What do you mean?" said the other.

"I mean it'll get its little neck wrung," said the Third.

"Well, we'll see," said Gannett. "I shall know what to think if it does die."

"I shall never see that bird again," said Rogers, shaking his head as the Chief took up the cage and handed it to the steward, who was to accompany him home with it.

The couple left the ship and proceeded down the East India Dock Road side by side, the only incident being a hot argument between a constable and the engineer as to whether he could or could not be held responsible for the language in which the parrot saw fit to indulge when the steward happened to drop it.

The engineer took the cage at his door, and, not without some misgivings, took it upstairs into the parlour and set it on the table. Mrs. Gannett, a simple-looking woman, with sleepy brown eyes and a docile manner, clapped her hands with joy.

"Isn't it a beauty?" said Mr. Gannett, looking at it; "I bought it to be company for you while I'm away."

"You're too good to me, Jem," said his wife. She walked all round the cage admiring it, the parrot, which was of a highly suspicious and nervous disposition, having had boys at its last place, turning with her. After she had walked round him five times he got sick of it, and in a simple sailorly fashion said so.

"Oh, Jem," said his wife.

"It's a beautiful talker," said Gannett hastily, "and it's so clever that it picks up everything it hears, but it'll soon forget it."

"It looks as though it knows what you are saying," said his wife. "Just look at it, the artful thing."

The opportunity was too good to be missed, and in a few straightforward lies the engineer acquainted Mrs. Gannett of the miraculous powers with which he had chosen to endow it.

"But you don't believe it?" said his wife, staring at him open-mouthed.

"I do," said the engineer firmly.

"But how can it know what I'm doing when I'm away?" persisted Mrs. Gannett.

"Ah, that's its secret," said the engineer; "a good many people would like to know that, but nobody has found out yet. It's a magic bird, and when you've said that you've said all there is to say about it."

Mrs. Gannett, wrinkling her forehead, eyed the marvellous bird curiously.

"You'll find it's quite true," said Gannett; "when I come back that bird'll be able to tell me how you've been and all about you. Everything you've done during my absence."

"Good gracious!" said the astonished Mrs. Gannett.

"If you stay out after seven of an evening, or do anything else that I shouldn't like, that bird'll tell me," continued the engineer impressively. "It'll tell me who comes to see you, and in fact it will tell me everything you do while I'm away."

"Well, it won't have anything bad to tell of me," said Mrs. Gannett composedly, "unless tells lies."

"It can't tell lies," said her husband confidently, "and now, if you go and put your bonnet on, we'll drop in at the theatre for half an hour."

It was a prophetic utterance, for he made such a fuss over the man next to his wife offering her his opera-glasses, that they left, at the urgent request of the management, in almost exactly that space of time.

"You'd better carry me about in a bandbox," said Mrs. Gannett wearily as the outraged engineer stalked home beside her. "What harm was the man doing?"

"You must have given him some encouragement," said Mr. Gannett fiercely—"made eyes at him or something. A man wouldn't offer to lend a lady his opera-glasses without."

Mrs. Gannett tossed her head—and that so decidedly, that a passing stranger turned his head and looked at her. Mr. Gannett accelerated his pace, and taking his wife's arm, led her swiftly home with a passion too great for words.

By the morning his anger had evaporated, but his misgivings remained. He left after breakfast for the Curlew, which was to sail in the afternoon, leaving behind him copious instructions, by following which his wife would be enabled to come down and see him off with the minimum exposure of her fatal charms.

Left to herself Mrs. Gannett dusted the room, until, coming to the parrot's cage, she put down the duster and eyed its eerie occupant curiously. She fancied that she saw an evil glitter in the creature's eye, and the knowing way in which it drew the film over it was as near an approach to a wink as a bird could get.

She was still looking at it when there was a knock at the door, and a bright little woman—rather smartly dressed—bustled into the room, and greeted her effusively.

"I just came to see you, my dear, because I thought a little outing would do me good," she said briskly; "and if you've no objection I'll come down to the docks with you to see the boat off."

Mrs. Gannett assented readily. It would ease the engineer's mind, she thought, if he saw her with a chaperon.

"Nice bird," said Mrs. Cluffins, mechanically bringing her parasol to the charge.

"Don't do that," said her friend hastily.

"Why not?" said the other.

"Language!" said Mrs. Gannett solemnly.

"Well, I must do something to it," said Mrs. Cluffins restlessly.

She held the parasol near the cage and suddenly opened it. It was a flaming scarlet, and for the moment the shock took the parrot's breath away.

"He don't mind that," said Mrs. Gannett.

The parrot, hopping to the farthest corner of the bottom of his cage, said something feebly. Finding that nothing dreadful happened, he repeated his remark somewhat more boldly, and, being convinced after all that the apparition was quite harmless and that he had displayed his craven spirit for nothing, hopped back on his perch and raved wickedly.

"If that was my bird," said Mrs. Cluffins, almost as scarlet as her parasol, "I should wring its neck."

"No, you wouldn't," said Mrs. Gannett solemnly. And having quieted the bird by throwing a cloth over its cage, she explained its properties.

"What!" said Mrs. Cluffins, unable to sit still in her chair. "You mean to tell me your husband said that!"

Mrs. Gannett nodded.

"He's awfully jealous of me," she said with a slight simper.

"I wish he was my husband," said Mrs. Cluffins in a thin, hard voice. "I wish C. would talk to me like that I wish somebody would try and persuade C. to talk to me like that."

"It shows he's fond of me," said Mrs. Gannett, looking down.

Mrs. Cluffins jumped up, and snatching the cover off the cage, endeavoured, but in vain, to get the parasol through the bars.

"And you believe that rubbish!" she said scathingly. "Boo, you wretch!"

"I don't believe it," said her friend, taking her gently away and covering the cage hastily just as the bird was recovering, "but I let him think I do."

"I call it an outrage," said Mrs. Cluffins, waving the parasol wildly. "I never heard of such a thing; I'd like to give Mr. Gannett a piece of my mind. Just about half an hour of it. He wouldn't be the same man afterwards—I'd parrot him."

Mrs. Gannett, soothing her agitated friend as well as she was able, led her gently to a chair and removed her bonnet, and finding that complete recovery was impossible while the parrot remained in the room, took that wonder-working bird outside.

By the time they had reached the docks and boarded the Curlew Mrs. Cluffins had quite recovered her spirits. She roamed about the steamer asking questions, which savoured more of idle curiosity than a genuine thirst for knowledge, and was at no pains to conceal her opinion of those who were unable to furnish her with satisfactory replies.

"I shall think of you every day, Jem," said Mrs. Gannett tenderly.

"I shall think of you every minute," said the engineer reproachfully.

He sighed gently and gazed in a scandalised fashion at Mrs. Cluffins, who was carrying on a desperate flirtation with one of the apprentices.

"She's very light-hearted," said his wife, following the direction of his eyes.

"She is," said Mr. Gannett curtly, as the unconscious Mrs. Cluffins shut her parasol and rapped the apprentice playfully with the handle. "She seems to be on very good terms with Jenkins, laughing and carrying on. I don't suppose she's ever seen him before."

"Poor young things," said Mrs. Cluffins solemnly, as she came up to them. "Don't you worry, Mr. Gannett; I'll look after her and keep her from moping."

"You're very kind," said the engineer slowly.

"We'll have a jolly time," said Mrs. Cluffins. "I often wish my husband was a seafaring man. A wife does have more freedom, doesn't she?"

"More what?" inquired Mr. Gannett huskily.

"More freedom," said Mrs. Cluffins gravely. "I always envy sailors' wives. They can do as they like. No husband to look after them for nine or ten months in the year."

Before the unhappy engineer could put his indignant thoughts into words there was a warning cry from the gangway, and with a hasty farewell he hurried below. The visitors went ashore, the gangway was shipped, and in response to the clang of the telegraph the Curlew drifted slowly away from the quay and headed for the swing-bridge slowly opening in front of her.

The two ladies hurried to the pier-head and watched the steamer down the river until a bend hid it from view. Then Mrs. Gannett, with a sensation of having lost something, due, so her friend assured her, to the want of a cup of tea, went slowly back to her lonely home.

In the period of grass-widowhood which ensued, Mrs. Cluffins's visits formed almost the sole relief to the bare monotony of existence. As a companion the parrot was an utter failure, its language being so irredeemably bad that it spent most of its time in the spare room with a cloth over its cage, wondering when the days were going to lengthen a bit. Mrs. Cluffins suggested selling it, but her friend repelled the suggestion with horror, and refused to entertain it at any price, even that of the publican at the corner, who, having heard of the bird's command of language, was bent upon buying it.

"I wonder what that beauty will have to tell your husband," said Mrs. Cluffins, as they sat together one day some three months after the Curlew's departure.

"I should hope that he has forgotten that nonsense," said Mrs. Gannett, reddening; "he never alludes to it in his letters."

"Sell it," said Mrs. Cluffins peremptorily. "It's no good to you, and Hobson would give anything for it almost."

Mrs. Gannett shook her head. "The house wouldn't hold my husband if I did," she remarked with a shiver.

"Oh, yes, it would," said Mrs. Cluffins; "you do as I tell you, and a much smaller house than this would hold him. I told C. to tell Hobson he should have it for five pounds."

"But he mustn't," said her friend in alarm.

"Leave yourself right in my hands," said Mrs. Cluffins, spreading out two small palms and regarding them complacently. "It'll be all right, I promise you."

She put her arm round her friend's waist and led her to the window, talking earnestly. In five minutes Mrs. Gannett was wavering, in ten she had given way, and in fifteen the energetic Mrs. Cluffins was en route for Hobson's, swinging the cage so violently in her excitement that the parrot was reduced to holding on to its perch with claws and bill. Mrs. Gannett watched the progress from the window, and with a queer look on her face sat down to think out the points of attack and defence in the approaching fray.

A week later a four-wheeler drove up to the door, and the engineer, darting upstairs three steps at a time, dropped an armful of parcels on the floor, and caught his wife in an embrace which would have done credit to a bear. Mrs. Gannett, for reasons of which lack of muscle was only one, responded less ardently.

"Ha, it's good to be home again," said Gannett, sinking into an easy-chair and pulling his wife on his knee. "And how have you been? Lonely?"

"I got used to it," said Mrs. Gannett softly.

The engineer coughed. "You had the parrot," he remarked.

"Yes, I had the magic parrot," said Mrs. Gannett.

"How's it getting on?" said her husband, looking round. "Where is it?"

"Part of it is on the mantelpiece," said Mrs. Gannett, trying to speak calmly, "part of it is in a bonnet-box upstairs, some of it's in my pocket, and here is the remainder."

She fumbled in her pocket and placed in his hand a cheap two-bladed clasp knife.

"On the mantelpiece!" repeated the engineer staring at the knife; "in a bonnet-box!" "Those blue vases," said his wife. Mr. Gannett put his hand to his head. If he had heard aright one parrot had changed into a pair of vases, a bonnet, and a knife. A magic bird with a vengeance.

"I sold it," said Mrs. Gannett suddenly.

The engineer's knee stiffened inhospitably, and his arm dropped from his wife's waist She rose quietly and took a chair opposite.

"Sold it!" said Mr. Gannett in awful tones. "Sold my parrot!"

"I didn't like it, Jem," said his wife. "I didn't want that bird watching me, and I did want the vases, and the bonnet, and the little present for you."

Mr. Gannett pitched the little present to the other end of the room.

"You see it mightn't have told the truth, Jem," continued Mrs. Gannett. "It might have told all sorts of lies about me, and made no end of mischief."

"It couldn't lie," shouted the engineer passionately, rising from his chair and pacing the room. "It's your guilty conscience that's made a coward of you. How dare you sell my parrot?"

"Because it wasn't truthful, Jem," said his wife, who was somewhat pale.

"If you were half as truthful you'd do," vociferated the engineer, standing over her. "You, you deceitful woman."

Mrs. Gannett fumbled in her pocket again, and producing a small handkerchief applied it delicately to her eyes.

"I—I got rid of it for your sake," she stammered. "It used to tell such lies about you. I couldn't bear to listen to it."

"About me!" said Mr. Gannett, sinking into his seat and staring at his wife with very natural amazement. "Tell lies about me! Nonsense! How could it?"

"I suppose it could tell me about you as easily as it could tell you about me?" said Mrs. Gannett. "There was more magic in that bird than you thought, Jem. It used to say shocking things about you. I couldn't bear it."

"Do you think you're talking to a child or a fool?" demanded the engineer.

Mrs. Gannett shook her head feebly. She still kept the handkerchief to her eyes, but allowed a portion to drop over her mouth.

"I should like to hear some of the stories it told about me—if you can remember them," said the engineer with bitter sarcasm.

"The first lie," said Mrs. Gannett in a feeble but ready voice, "was about the time you were at Genoa. The parrot said you were at some concert gardens at the upper end of the town."

One moist eye coming mildly from behind the handkerchief saw the engineer stiffen suddenly in his chair.

"I don't suppose there even is such a place," she continued.

"I—b'leve—there—is," said her husband jerkily. "I've heard—our chaps—talk of it."

"But you haven't been there?" said his wife anxiously.

"Never!" said the engineer with extraordinary vehemence.

"That wicked bird said that you got intoxicated there," said Mrs. Gannett in solemn accents, "that you smashed a little marble-topped table and knocked down two waiters, and that if it hadn't been for the captain of the Pursuit, who was in there and who got you away, you'd have been locked up. Wasn't it a wicked bird?"

"Horrible!" said the engineer huskily.

"I don't suppose there ever was a ship called the Pursuit," continued Mrs. Gannett.

"Doesn't sound like a ship's name," murmured Mr. Gannett.

"Well, then, a few days later it said the Curlew was at Naples."

"I never went ashore all the time we were at Naples," remarked the engineer casually.

"The parrot said you did," said Mrs. Gannett.

"I suppose you'll believe your own lawful husband before that damned bird?" shouted Gannett, starting up.

"Of course I didn't believe it, Jem," said his wife. "I'm trying to prove to you that the bird was not truthful, but you're so hard to persuade."

Mr. Gannett took a pipe from his pocket, and with a small knife dug with much severity and determination a hardened plug from the bowl, and blew noisily through the stem.

"There was a girl kept a fruit-stall just by the harbour," said Mrs. Gannett, "and on this evening, on the strength of having bought three-pennyworth of green figs, you put your arm round her waist and tried to kiss her, and her sweetheart, who was standing close by, tried to stab you. The parrot said that you were in such a state of terror that you jumped into the harbour and were nearly drowned."

Mr. Gannett having loaded his pipe lit it slowly and carefully, and with tidy precision got up and deposited the match in the fireplace.

"It used to frighten me so with its stories that I hardly knew what to do with myself," continued Mrs. Gannett "When you were at Suez—"

The engineer waved his hand imperiously.

"That's enough," he said stiffly.

"I'm sure I don't want to have to repeat what it told me about Suez," said his wife. "I thought you'd like to hear it, that's all."

"Not at all," said the engineer, puffing at his pipe. "Not at all."

"But you see why I got rid of the bird, don't you?" said Mrs. Gannett. "If it had told you untruths about me, you would have believed them, wouldn't you?"

Mr. Gannett took his pipe from his mouth and took his wife in his extended arms. "No, my dear," he said brokenly, "no more than you believe all this stuff about me."

"And I did quite right to sell it, didn't I, Jem?"

"Quite right," said Mr. Gannett with a great assumption of heartiness. "Best thing to do with it."

"You haven't heard the worst yet," said Mrs. Gannett. "When you were at Suez—"

Mr. Gannett consigned Suez to its only rival, and thumping the table with his clenched fist, forbade his wife to mention the word again, and desired her to prepare supper.

Not until he heard his wife moving about in the kitchen below did he relax the severity of his countenance. Then his expression changed to one of extreme anxiety, and he restlessly paced the room seeking for light. It came suddenly.

"Jenkins," he gasped, "Jenkins and Mrs. Cluffins, and I was going to tell Cluffins about him writing to his wife. I expect he knows the letter by heart."

The night-watchman shook his head. "I never met any of these phil— philantherpists, as you call 'em," he said, decidedly. "If I 'ad they wouldn't 'ave got away from me in a hurry, I can tell you. I don't say I don't believe in 'em; I only say I never met any of 'em. If people do you a kindness it's generally because they want to get something out of you; same as a man once—a perfick stranger— wot stood me eight 'arf-pints becos I reminded 'im of his dead brother, and then borrered five bob off of me.

"O' course, there must be some kind-'arted people in the world—all men who get married must 'ave a soft spot somewhere, if it's only in the 'ead—but they don't often give things away. Kind-'artedness is often only another name for artfulness, same as Sam Small's kindness to Ginger Dick and Peter Russet.

"It started with a row. They was just back from a v'y'ge and 'ad taken a nice room together in Wapping, and for the fust day or two, wot with 'aving plenty o' money to spend and nothing to do, they was like three brothers. Then, in a little, old-fashioned public-'ouse down Poplar way, one night they fell out over a little joke Ginger played on Sam.

"It was the fust drink that evening, and Sam 'ad just ordered a pot o' beer and three glasses, when Ginger winked at the landlord and offered to bet Sam a level 'arf-dollar that 'e wouldn't drink off that pot o' beer without taking breath. The landlord held the money, and old Sam, with a 'appy smile on 'is face, 'ad just taken up the mug, when he noticed the odd way in which they was all watching him. Twice he took the mug up and put it down agin without starting and asked 'em wot the little game was, but they on'y laughed. He took it up the third time and started, and he 'ad just got about 'arf-way through when Ginger turns to the landlord and ses—

"'Did you catch it in the mouse-trap,' he ses, 'or did it die of poison?'

"Pore Sam started as though he 'ad been shot, and, arter getting rid of the beer in 'is mouth, stood there 'olding the mug away from 'im and making such 'orrible faces that they was a'most frightened.

"'Wot's the matter with him? I've never seen 'im carry on like that over a drop of beer before,' ses Ginger, staring.

"'He usually likes it,' ses Peter Russet.

"'Not with a dead mouse in it,' ses Sam, trembling with passion.

"'Mouse?' ses Ginger, innercent-like. 'Mouse? Why, I didn't say it was in your beer, Sam. Wotever put that into your 'ead?'

"'And made you lose your bet,' ses Peter.

"Then old Sam see 'ow he'd been done, and the way he carried on when the landlord gave Ginger the 'arf-dollar, and said it was won fair and honest, was a disgrace. He 'opped about that bar 'arf crazy, until at last the landlord and 'is brother, and a couple o' soldiers, and a helpless cripple wot wos selling matches, put 'im outside and told 'im to stop there.

"He stopped there till Ginger and Peter came out, and then, drawing 'imself up in a proud way, he told 'em their characters and wot he thought about 'em. And he said 'e never wanted to see wot they called their faces agin as long as he lived.

"'I've done with you,' he ses, 'both of you, forever.'

"'All right,' ses Ginger moving off. 'Ta-ta for the present. Let's 'ope he'll come 'ome in a better temper, Peter.'

"'Ome?' ses Sam, with a nasty laugh, "'ome? D'ye think I'm coming back to breathe the same air as you, Ginger? D'ye think I want to be suffocated?'

"He held his 'ead up very 'igh, and, arter looking at them as if they was dirt, he turned round and walked off with his nose in the air to spend the evening by 'imself.

"His temper kept him up for a time, but arter a while he 'ad to own up to 'imself that it was very dull, and the later it got the more he thought of 'is nice warm bed. The more 'e thought of it the nicer and warmer it seemed, and, arter a struggle between his pride and a few 'arf-pints, he got 'is good temper back agin and went off 'ome smiling.

"The room was dark when 'e got there, and, arter standing listening a moment to Ginger and Peter snoring, he took off 'is coat and sat down on 'is bed to take 'is boots off. He only sat down for a flash, and then he bent down and hit his 'ead an awful smack against another 'ead wot 'ad just started up to see wot it was sitting on its legs.

"He thought it was Peter or Ginger in the wrong bed at fust, but afore he could make it out Ginger 'ad got out of 'is own bed and lit the candle. Then 'e saw it was a stranger in 'is bed, and without saying a word he laid 'old of him by the 'air and began dragging him out.

"'Here, stop that!' ses Ginger catching hold of 'im. 'Lend a hand 'ere, Peter.'

"Peter lent a hand and screwed it into the back o' Sam's neck till he made 'im leave go, and then the stranger, a nasty-looking little chap with a yellow face and a little dark moustache, told Sam wot he'd like to do to him.

"'Who are you?' ses Sam, 'and wot are you a-doing of in my bed?'

"'It's our lodger,' ses Ginger.

"'Your wot?' ses Sam, 'ardly able to believe his ears.

"'Our lodger,' ses Peter Russet. 'We've let 'im the bed you said you didn't want for sixpence a night. Now you take yourself off.'

"Old Sam couldn't speak for a minute; there was no words that he knew bad enough, but at last he licks 'is lips and he ses, 'I've paid for that bed up to Saturday, and I'm going to have it.'

"He rushed at the lodger, but Peter and Ginger got hold of 'im agin and put 'im down on the floor and sat on 'im till he promised to be'ave himself. They let 'im get up at last, and then, arter calling themselves names for their kind-'artedness, they said if he was very good he might sleep on the floor.

"Sam looked at 'em for a moment, and then, without a word, he took off 'is boots and put on 'is coat and went up in a corner to be out of the draught, but, wot with the cold and 'is temper, and the hardness of the floor, it was a long time afore 'e could get to sleep. He dropped off at last, and it seemed to 'im that he 'ad only just closed 'is eyes when it was daylight. He opened one eye and was just going to open the other when he saw something as made 'im screw 'em both up sharp and peep through 'is eyelashes. The lodger was standing at the foot o' Ginger's bed, going through 'is pockets, and then, arter waiting a moment and 'aving a look round, he went through Peter Russet's. Sam lay still mouse while the lodger tip-toed out o' the room with 'is boots in his 'and, and then, springing up, follered him downstairs.

"He caught 'im up just as he 'ad undone the front door, and, catching hold of 'im by the back o' the neck, shook 'im till 'e was tired. Then he let go of 'im and, holding his fist under 'is nose, told 'im to hand over the money, and look sharp about it.

"'Ye—ye—yes, sir,' ses the lodger, who was 'arf choked.

"Sam held out his 'and, and the lodger, arter saying it was only a little bit o' fun on 'is part, and telling 'im wot a fancy he 'ad taken to 'im from the fust, put Ginger's watch and chain into his 'ands and eighteen pounds four shillings and sevenpence. Sam put it into his pocket, and, arter going through the lodger's pockets to make sure he 'adn't forgot anything, opened the door and flung 'im into the street. He stopped on the landing to put the money in a belt he was wearing under 'is clothes, and then 'e went back on tip-toe to 'is corner and went to sleep with one eye open and the 'appiest smile that had been on his face for years.

"He shut both eyes when he 'eard Ginger wake up, and he slept like a child through the 'orrible noise that Peter and Ginger see fit to make when they started to put their clothes on. He got tired of it afore they did, and, arter opening 'is eyes slowly and yawning, he asked Ginger wot he meant by it.

"'You'll wake your lodger up if you ain't careful, making that noise,' he ses. 'Wot's the matter?'

"'Sam,' ses Ginger, in a very different voice to wot he 'ad used the night before, 'Sam, old pal, he's taken all our money and bolted.'

"'Wot?' ses Sam, sitting up on the floor and blinking, 'Nonsense!'

"'Robbed me and Peter,' ses Ginger, in a trembling voice; 'taken every penny we've got, and my watch and chain.'

"'You're dreaming,' ses Sam.

"'I wish I was,' ses Ginger.

"'But surely, Ginger,' ses Sam, standing up, 'surely you didn't take a lodger without a character?'

"'He seemed such a nice chap,' ses Peter. 'We was only saying wot a much nicer chap he was than—than—'

"'Go on, Peter,' ses Sam, very perlite.

"'Than he might ha' been,' ses Ginger, very quick.

"'Well, I've 'ad a wonderful escape,' ses Sam. 'If it hadn't ha' been for sleeping in my clothes I suppose he'd ha' 'ad my money as well.'

"He felt in 'is pockets anxious-like, then he smiled, and stood there letting 'is money fall through 'is fingers into his pocket over and over agin.

"'Pore chap,' he ses; 'pore chap; p'r'aps he'd got a starving wife and family. Who knows? It ain't for us to judge 'im, Ginger.'

"He stood a little while longer chinking 'is money, and when he took off his coat to wash Ginger Dick poured the water out for im and Peter Russet picked up the soap, which 'ad fallen on the floor. Then they started pitying themselves, looking very 'ard at the back of old Sam while they did it.

"'I s'pose we've got to starve, Peter,' ses Ginger, in, a sad voice.

"'Looks like it,' ses Peter, dressing hisself very slowly.

"'There's nobody'll mourn for me, that's one comfort,' ses Ginger.

"'Or me,' ses Peter.

"'P'r'aps Sam'll miss us a bit,' ses Ginger, grinding 'is teeth as old Sam went on washing as if he was deaf. 'He'ss the only real pal we ever 'ad.'

"'Wot are you talking about?' ses Sam, turning round with the soap in his eyes, and feeling for the towel. 'Wot d'ye want to starve for? Why don't you get a ship?'

"'I thought we was all going to sign on in the Cheaspeake agin, Sam,' ses Ginger, very mild.

"'She won't be ready for sea for pretty near three weeks,' ses Sam. 'You know that.'

"'P'r'aps Sam would lend us a trifle to go on with, Ginger,' ses Peter Russet. 'Just enough to keep body and soul together, so as we can hold out and 'ave the pleasure of sailing with 'im agin.'

"'P'r'aps he wouldn't,' ses Sam, afore Ginger could open his mouth. 'I've just got about enough to last myself; I 'aven't got any to lend. Sailormen wot turns on their best friends and makes them sleep on the cold 'ard floor while their new pal is in his bed don't get money lent to 'em. My neck is so stiff it creaks every time I move it, and I've got the rheumatics in my legs something cruel.'

"He began to 'um a song, and putting on 'is cap went out to get some brekfuss. He went to a little eating-'ouse near by, where they was in the 'abit of going, and 'ad just started on a plate of eggs and bacon when Ginger Dick and Peter came into the place with a pocket-'ankercher of 'is wot they 'ad found in the fender.

"'We thought you might want it, Sam,' ses Peter.

"'So we brought it along,' ses Ginger. 'I 'ope you're enjoying of your brekfuss, Sam.'

"Sam took the 'ankercher and thanked 'em very perlite, and arter standing there for a minute or two as if they wanted to say something they couldn't remember, they sheered off. When Sam left the place 'arf-an-hour afterwards they was still hanging about, and as Sam passed Ginger asked 'im if he was going for a walk.

"'Walk?' ses Sam. 'Cert'nly not. I'm going to bed; I didn't 'ave a good night's rest like you and your lodger.'

"He went back 'ome, and arter taking off 'is coat and boots got into bed and slept like a top till one o'clock, when he woke up to find Ginger shaking 'im by the shoulders.

"'Wot's the matter?' he ses. 'Wot are you up to?'

"'It's dinner-time,' ses Ginger. 'I thought p'r'aps you'd like to know, in case you missed it.'

"'You leave me alone,' ses Sam, cuddling into the clothes agin. 'I don't want no dinner. You go and look arter your own dinners.'

"He stayed in bed for another 'arf-hour, listening to Peter and Ginger telling each other in loud whispers 'ow hungry they was, and then he got up and put 'is things on and went to the door.

"'I'm going to get a bit o' dinner,' he ses. 'And mind, I've got my pocket 'ankercher.'

"He went out and 'ad a steak and onions and a pint o' beer, but, although he kept looking up sudden from 'is plate, he didn't see Peter or Ginger. It spoilt 'is dinner a bit, but arter he got outside 'e saw them standing at the corner, and, pretending not to see them, he went off for a walk down the Mile End Road.

"He walked as far as Bow with them follering 'im, and then he jumped on a bus and rode back as far as Whitechapel. There was no sign of 'em when he got off, and, feeling a bit lonesome, he stood about looking in shop-windows until 'e see them coming along as hard as they could come.

"'Why, halloa!' he ses. 'Where did you spring from?'

"'We—we—we've been—for a bit of a walk,' ses Ginger Dick, puffing and blowing like a grampus.

"'To-keep down the 'unger,' ses Peter Russet.

"Old Sam looked at 'em very stern for a moment, then he beckoned 'em to foller 'im, and, stopping at a little public-'ouse, he went in and ordered a pint o' bitter.

"'And give them two pore fellers a crust o' bread and cheese and 'arf-a-pint of four ale each,' he ses to the barmaid.

"Ginger and Peter looked at each other, but they was so hungry they didn't say a word; they just stood waiting.

"'Put that inside you my pore fellers,' ses Sam, with a oily smile. 'I can't bear to see people suffering for want o' food,' he ses to the barmaid, as he chucked down a sovereign on the counter.

"The barmaid, a very nice gal with black 'air and her fingers covered all over with rings, said that it did 'im credit, and they stood there talking about tramps and beggars and such-like till Peter and Ginger nearly choked. He stood there watching 'em and smoking a threepenny cigar, and when they 'ad finished he told the barmaid to give 'em a sausage-roll each, and went off.

"Peter and Ginger snatched up their sausage-rolls and follered 'im, and at last Ginger swallowed his pride and walked up to 'im and asked 'im to lend them some money.

"'You'll get it back agin,' he ses. 'You know that well enough.'

"'Cert'nly not,' ses Sam; 'and I'm surprised at you asking. Why, a child could rob you. It's 'ard enough as it is for a pore man like me to 'ave to keep a couple o' hulking sailormen, but I'm not going to give you money to chuck away on lodgers. No more sleeping on the floor for me! Now I don't want none o' your langwidge, and I don't want you follering me like a couple o' cats arter a meat-barrer. I shall be 'aving a cup o' tea at Brown's coffee-shop by and by, and if you're there at five sharp I'll see wot I can do for you. Wot did you call me?'

"Ginger told 'im three times, and then Peter Russet dragged 'im away. They turned up outside Brown's at a quarter to five, and at ten past six Sam Small strolled up smoking a cigar, and, arter telling them that he 'ad forgot all about 'em, took 'em inside and paid for their teas. He told Mr. Brown 'e was paying for 'em, and 'e told the gal wot served 'em 'e was paying for 'em, and it was all pore Ginger could do to stop 'imself from throwing his plate in 'is face.

"Sam went off by 'imself, and arter walking about all the evening without a ha'penny in their pockets, Ginger Dick and Peter went off 'ome to bed and went to sleep till twelve o'clock, when Sam came in and woke 'em up to tell 'em about a music-'all he 'ad been to, and 'ow many pints he had 'ad. He sat up in bed till past one o'clock talking about 'imself, and twice Peter Russet woke Ginger up to listen and got punched for 'is trouble.

"They both said they'd get a ship next morning, and then old Sam turned round and wouldn't 'ear of it. The airs he gave 'imself was awful. He said he'd tell 'em when they was to get a ship, and if they went and did things without asking 'im he'd let 'em starve.

"He kept 'em with 'im all that day for fear of losing 'em and having to give 'em their money when 'e met 'em agin instead of spending it on 'em and getting praised for it. They 'ad their dinner with 'im at Brown's, and nothing they could do pleased him. He spoke to Peter Russet out loud about making a noise while he was eating, and directly arterwards he told Ginger to use his pocket 'ankercher. Pore Ginger sat there looking at 'im and swelling and swelling until he nearly bust, and Sam told 'im if he couldn't keep 'is temper when people was trying to do 'im a kindness he'd better go and get somebody else to keep him.

"He took 'em to a music-'all that night, but he spoilt it all for 'em by taking 'em into the little public-'ouse in Whitechapel Road fust and standing 'em a drink. He told the barmaid 'e was keeping 'em till they could find a job, and arter she 'ad told him he was too soft-'arted and would only be took advantage of, she brought another barmaid up to look at 'em and ask 'em wot they could do, and why they didn't do it.

"Sam served 'em like that for over a week, and he 'ad so much praise from Mr. Brown and other people that it nearly turned his 'ead. For once in his life he 'ad it pretty near all 'is own way. Twice Ginger Dick slipped off and tried to get a ship and came back sulky and hungry, and once Peter Russet sprained his thumb trying to get a job at the docks.

"They gave it up then and kept to Sam like a couple o' shadders, only giving 'im back-answers when they felt as if something 'ud give way inside if they didn't. For the fust time in their lives they began to count the days till their boat was ready for sea. Then something happened.

"They was all coming 'ome late one night along the Minories, when Ginger Dick gave a shout and, suddenly bolting up a little street arter a man that 'ad turned up there, fust of all sent 'im flying with a heavy punch of 'is fist, and then knelt on 'im.

"'Now then Ginger,' ses Sam bustling up with Peter Russet, 'wot's all this? Wot yer doing?'

"'It's the thief,' ses Ginger. 'It's our lodger. You keep still!' he ses shaking the man. 'D'ye hear?'

"Peter gave a shout of joy, and stood by to help.

"'Nonsense!' ses old Sam, turning pale. 'You've been drinking, Ginger. This comes of standing you 'arf-pints.'

"'It's him right enough,' ses Ginger. 'I'd know 'is ugly face anywhere.'

"'You come off 'ome at once,' ses Sam, very sharp, but his voice trembling. 'At once. D'ye hear me?'

"'Fetch a policeman, Peter,' ses Ginger.

"'Let the pore feller go, I tell you,' ses Sam, stamping his foot. "Ow would you like to be locked up? 'Ow would you like to be torn away from your wife and little ones? 'Ow would you—'

"'Fetch a policeman, Peter,' ses Ginger agin. 'D'ye hear?'

"'Don't do that, guv'nor,' ses the lodger. 'You got your money back. Wot's the good o' putting me away?'

"'Got our wot back?' ses Ginger, shaking 'im agin. 'Don't you try and be funny with me, else I'll tear you into little pieces.'

"'But he took it back,' ses the man, trying to sit up and pointing at Sam. 'He follered me downstairs and took it all away from me. Your ticker as well.'

"'Wot?' ses Ginger and Peter both together.

"Strue as I'm 'ere,' ses the lodger. 'You turn 'is pockets out and see. Look out! He's going off!'

"Ginger turned his 'ead just in time to see old Sam nipping round the corner. He pulled the lodger up like a flash, and, telling Peter to take hold of the other side of him, they set off arter Sam.

"'Little-joke-o' mine-Ginger,' ses Sam, when they caught 'im. 'I was going to tell you about it to-night. It ain't often I get the chance of a joke agin you Ginger; you're too sharp for a old man like me.'

"Ginger Dick didn't say anything. He kept 'old o' Sam's arm with one hand and the lodger's neck with the other, and marched 'em off to his lodgings.

"He shut the door when 'e got in, and arter Peter 'ad lit the candle they took hold o' Sam and went through 'im, and arter trying to find pockets where he 'adn't got any, they took off 'is belt and found Ginger's watch, seventeen pounds five shillings, and a few coppers.

"'We 'ad over nine quid each, me and Peter,' ses Ginger. 'Where's the rest?'

"'It's all I've got left,' ses Sam; 'every ha'penny.'

"He 'ad to undress and even take 'is boots off afore they'd believe 'im, and then Ginger took 'is watch and he ses to Peter, 'Lemme see; 'arf of seventeen pounds is eight pounds ten; 'arf of five shillings is 'arf-a-crown; and 'arf of fourpence is twopence.'

"'What about me Ginger old pal?' ses Sam, in a kind voice. 'We must divide it into threes.'

"'Threes?' ses Ginger, staring at'im. 'Whaffor?'

"''Cos part of it's mine,' ses Sam, struggling 'ard to be perlite. 'I've paid for everything for the last ten days, ain't I?'

"'Yes,' ses Ginger. 'You 'ave, and I thank you for it.'

"'So do I,' ses Peter Russet. 'Hearty I do.'

"'It was your kind-'artedness,' ses Ginger, grinning like mad. 'You gave it to us, and we wouldn't dream of giving it to you back.'

"'Nothin' o' the kind,' ses Sam, choking.

"'Oh, yes you did,' ses Ginger, 'and you didn't forget to tell people neither. You told everybody. Now it's our turn.'

"He opened the door and kicked the lodger out. Leastways, he would 'ave kicked 'im, but the chap was too quick for 'im. And then 'e came back, and, putting his arm round Peter's waist, danced a waltz round the room with 'im, while pore old Sam got on to his bed to be out of the way. They danced for nearly 'arf-an-hour, and then they undressed and sat on Peter's bed and talked. They talked in whispers at fust, but at last Sam 'eard Peter say:—

"'Threepence for 'is brekfuss; sevenpence for 'is dinner; threepence for 'is tea; penny for beer and a penny for bacca. 'Ow much is that, Ginger?'

"'One bob,' ses Ginger.

"Peter counted up to 'imself. 'I make it more than that, old pal,' he ses, when he 'ad finished.

"'Do you?' ses Ginger, getting up. 'Well, he won't; not if he counts it twenty times over he won't. Good-night, Peter. 'Appy dreams.'"

THE HEAD OF THE FAMILY

Mr. Letts had left his ship by mutual arrangement, and the whole of the crew had mustered to see him off and to express their sense of relief at his departure. After some years spent in long voyages, he had fancied a trip on a coaster as a change, and, the schooner Curlew having no use for a ship's carpenter, had shipped as cook. He had done his best, and the unpleasant epithets that followed him along the quay at Dunchurch as he followed in the wake of his sea-chest were the result. Master and mate nodded in grim appreciation of the crew's efforts.

He put his chest up at a seamen's lodging-house, and, by no means perturbed at this sudden change in his fortunes, sat on a seat overlooking the sea, with a cigarette between his lips, forming plans for his future. His eyes closed, and he opened them with a start to find that a middle-aged woman of pleasant but careworn appearance had taken the other end of the bench.

"Fine day," said Mr. Letts, lighting another cigarette.

The woman assented and sat looking over the sea.

"Ever done any cooking?" asked Mr. Letts, presently.

"Plenty," was the surprised reply. "Why?"

"I just wanted to ask you how long you would boil a bit o' beef," said Mr. Letts. "Only from curiosity; I should never ship as cook again."

He narrated his experience of the last few days, and, finding the listener sympathetic, talked at some length about himself and his voyages; also of his plans for the future.

"I lost my son at sea," said the woman, with a sigh. "You favor him rather."

Mr. Letts's face softened. "Sorry," he said. "Sorry you lost him, I mean."

"At least, I suppose he would have been like you," said the other; "but it's nine years ago now. He was just sixteen."

Mr. Letts—after a calculation—nodded. "Just my age," he said. "I was twenty-five last March."

"Sailed for Melbourne," said the woman. "My only boy."

Mr. Letts cleared his throat, sympathetically.

"His father died a week after he sailed," continued the other, "and three months afterwards my boy's ship went down. Two years ago, like a fool, I married again. I don't know why I'm talking to you like this. I suppose it is because you remind me of him."

"You talk away as much as you like," said Mr. Letts, kindly. "I've got nothing to do."

He lit another cigarette, and, sitting in an attitude of attention, listened to a recital of domestic trouble that made him congratulate himself upon remaining single.

"Since I married Mr. Green I can't call my soul my own," said the victim of matrimony as she rose to depart. "If my poor boy had lived things would have been different. His father left the house and furniture to him, and that's all my second married me for, I'm sure. That and the bit o' money that was left to me. He's selling some of my boy's furniture at this very moment. That's why I came out; I couldn't bear it."

"P'r'aps he'll turn up after all," said Mr. Letts. "Never say die."

Mrs. Green shook her head.

"I s'pose," said Mr. Letts, regarding her—"I s'pose you don't let lodgings for a night or two?" Mrs. Green shook her head again.

"It don't matter," said the young man. "Only I would sooner stay with you than at a lodging-house. I've taken a fancy to you. I say, it would be a lark if you did, and I went there and your husband thought I was your son, wouldn't it?"

Mrs. Green caught her breath, and sitting down again took his arm in her trembling fingers.

"Suppose," she said, unsteadily—"suppose you came round and pretended to be my son— pretended to be my son, and stood up for me?"

Mr. Letts stared at her in amazement, and then began to laugh.

"Nobody would know," continued the other, quickly. "We only came to this place just before he sailed, and his sister was only ten at the time. She wouldn't remember."

Mr. Letts said he couldn't think of it, and sat staring, with an air of great determination, at the sea. Arguments and entreaties left him unmoved, and he was just about to express his sorrow for her troubles and leave, when she gave a sudden start and put her arm through his.

"Here comes your sister!" she exclaimed.

Mr. Letts started in his turn.

"She has seen me holding your arm," continued Mrs. Green, in a tense whisper. "It's the only way I can explain it. Mind, your name is Jack Foster and hers is Betty."

Mr. Letts gazed at her in consternation, and then, raising his eyes, regarded with much approval the girl who was approaching. It seemed impossible that she could be Mrs. Green's daughter, and in the excitement of the moment he nearly said so.

"Betty," said Mrs. Green, in a voice to which nervousness had imparted almost the correct note— "Betty, this is your brother Jack!"

Mr. Letts rose sheepishly, and then to his great amazement a pair of strong young arms were flung round his neck, and a pair of warm lips— after but slight trouble—found his. Then and there Mr. Letts's mind was made up.

"Oh, Jack!" said Miss Foster, and began to cry softly.

"Oh, Jack!" said Mrs. Green, and, moved by thoughts, perhaps, of what might have been, began to cry too.

"There, there!" said Mr. Letts.

He drew Miss Foster to the seat, and, sitting between them, sat with an arm round each. There was nothing in sight but a sail or two in the far distance, and he allowed Miss Foster's head to lie upon his shoulder undisturbed. An only child, and an orphan, he felt for the first time the blessing of a sister's love.

"Why didn't you come home before?" murmured the girl.

Mr. Letts started and squinted reproachfully at the top of her hat. Then he turned and looked at Mrs. Green in search of the required information. "He was shipwrecked," said Mrs. Green.

"I was shipwrecked," repeated Mr. Letts, nodding.

"And had brain-fever after it through being in the water so long, and lost his memory," continued Mrs. Green.

"It's wonderful what water will do—salt water," said Mr. Letts, in confirmation.

Miss Foster sighed, and, raising the hand which was round her waist, bent her head and kissed it. Mr. Letts colored, and squeezed her convulsively.

Assisted by Mrs. Green he became reminiscent, and, in a low voice, narrated such incidents of his career as had escaped the assaults of the brain-fever. That his head was not permanently injured was proved by the perfect manner in which he remembered incidents of his childhood narrated by his newly found mother and sister. He even volunteered one or two himself which had happened when the latter was a year or two old.

"And now," said Mrs. Green, in a somewhat trembling voice, "we must go and tell your step-father."

Mr. Letts responded, but without briskness, and, with such moral support as an arm of each could afford, walked slowly back. Arrived at a road of substantial cottages at the back of the town, Mrs. Green gasped, and, coming to a standstill, nodded at a van that stood half-way up the road.

"There it is," she exclaimed.

"What?" demanded Mr. Letts.

"The furniture I told you about," said Mrs. Green. "The furniture that your poor father thought such a lot of, because it used to belong to his grandfather. He's selling it to Simpson, though I begged and prayed him not to."

Mr. Letts encouraged himself with a deep cough. "My furniture?" he demanded.

Mrs. Green took courage. "Yes," she said, hope-fully; "your father left it to you."

Mr. Letts, carrying his head very erect, took a firmer grip of their arms and gazed steadily at a disagreeable-looking man who was eying them in some astonishment from the doorway. With arms still linked they found the narrow gateway somewhat difficult, but they negotiated it by a turning movement, and, standing in the front garden, waited while Mrs. Green tried to find her voice.

"Jack," she said at last, "this is your stepfather."

Mr. Letts, in some difficulty as to the etiquette on such occasions, released his right arm and extended his hand.

"Good-evening, stepfather," he said, cheerfully.

Mr. Green drew back a little and regarded him unfavorably.

"We—we thought you was drowned," he said at last.

"I was nearly," said Mr. Letts.

"We all thought so," pursued Mr. Green, grudgingly. "Everybody thought so."

He stood aside, as a short, hot-faced man, with a small bureau clasped in his arms and supported on his knees, emerged from the house and staggered towards the gate. Mr. Letts reflected.

"Halloa!" he said, suddenly. "Why, are you moving, mother?"

Mrs. Green sniffed sadly and shook her head. "Well," said Mr. Letts, with an admirable stare, "what's that chap doing with my furniture?"

"Eh?" spluttered Mr. Green. "What?"

"I say, what's he doing with my furniture?" repeated Mr. Letts, sternly.

Mr. Green waved his arm. "That's all right," he said, conclusively; "he's bought it. Your mother knows."

"But it ain't all right," said Mr. Letts. "Here! bring that back, and those chairs too."

The dealer, who had just placed the bureau on the tail-board of the van, came back wiping his brow with his sleeve.

"Wots the little game?" he demanded.

Mr. Letts left the answer to Mr. Green, and going to the van took up the bureau and walked back to the house with it. Mr. Green and the dealer parted a little at his approach, and after widening the parting with the bureau he placed it in the front room while he went back for the chairs. He came back with three of them, and was, not without reason, called a porcupine by the indignant dealer.

He was relieved to find, after Mr. Simpson had taken his departure, that Mr. Green was in no mood for catechising him, and had evidently accepted the story of his escape and return as a particularly disagreeable fact. So disagreeable that the less he heard of it the better.

"I hope you've not come home after all these years to make things unpleasant?" he remarked presently, as they sat at tea.

"I couldn't be unpleasant if I tried," said Mr. Letts.

"We've been very happy and comfortable here—me and your mother and sister," continued Mr. Green. "Haven't we, Emily?"

"Yes," said his wife, with nervous quickness.

"And I hope you'll be the same," said Mr. Green. "It's my wish that you should make yourself quite comfortable here—till you go to sea again."

"Thankee," said Mr. Letts; "but I don't think I shall go to sea any more. Ship's carpenter is my trade, and I've been told more than once that I should do better ashore. Besides, I don't want to lose mother and Betty again."

He placed his arm round the girl's waist, and, drawing her head on to his shoulder, met with a blank stare the troubled gaze of Mrs. Green.

"I'm told there's wonderful openings for carpenters in Australia," said Mr. Green, trying to speak in level tones. "Wonderful! A good carpenter can make a fortune there in ten years, so I'm told."

Mr. Letts, with a slight wink at Mrs. Green and a reassuring squeeze with his left arm, turned an attentive ear.

"O' course, there's a difficulty," he said, slowly, as Mr. Green finished a vivid picture of the joys of carpentering in Australia.

"Difficulty?" said the other.

"Money to start with," explained Mr. Letts. "It's no good starting without money. I wonder how much this house and furniture would fetch? Is it all mine, mother?"

"M-m-most of it," stammered Mrs. Green, gazing in a fascinated fashion at the contorted visage of her husband.

"All except a chair in the kitchen and three stair-rods," said Betty.

"Speak when you're spoke to, miss!" snarled her stepfather. "When we married we mixed our furniture up together—mixed it up so that it would be impossible to tell which is which. Nobody could."

"For the matter o' that, you could have all the kitchen chairs and all the stair-rods," said Mr. Letts, generously. "However, I don't want to do anything in a hurry, and I shouldn't dream of going to Australia without Betty. It rests with her."

"She's going to be married," said Mr. Green, hastily; "and if she wasn't she wouldn't turn her poor, ailing mother out of house and home, that I'm certain of. She's not that sort. We've had a word or two at times—me and her—but I know a good daughter when I see one."

"Married?" echoed Mr. Letts, as his left arm relaxed its pressure. "Who to?"

"Young fellow o' the name of Henry Widden," replied Mr. Green, "a very steady young fellow; a great friend of mine."

"Oh!" said Mr. Letts, blankly.

"I'd got an idea, which I've been keeping as a little surprise," continued Mr. Green, speaking very rapidly, "of them living here with us, and saving house-rent and furniture."

Mr. Letts surveyed him with a dejected eye.

"It would be a fine start for them," continued the benevolent Mr. Green.

Mr. Letts, by a strong effort, regained his composure.

"I must have a look at him first," he said, briskly. "He mightn't meet with my approval."

"Eh?" said Mr. Green, starting. "Why, if Betty—"

"I must think it over," interrupted Mr. Letts, with a wave of his hand. "Betty is only nineteen, and, as head of the family, I don't think she can marry without my consent. I'm not sure, but I don't think so. Anyway, if she does, I won't have her husband here sitting in my chairs, eating off my tables, sleeping in my beds, wearing out my stair-rods, helping himself—"

"Stow it," said Miss Foster, calmly.

Mr. Letts started, and lost the thread of his discourse. "I must have a look at him," he concluded, lamely; "he may be all right, but then, again, he mightn't."

He finished his tea almost in silence, and, the meal over, emphasized his position as head of the family by taking the easy-chair, a piece of furniture sacred to Mr. Green, and subjecting that injured man to a catechism which strained his powers of endurance almost to breaking-point.

"Well, I sha'n't make any change at present," said Mr. Letts, when the task was finished. "There's plenty of room here for us all, and, so long as you and me agree, things can go on as they are. To-morrow morning I shall go out and look for a job."

He found a temporary one almost at once, and, determined to make a favorable impression, worked hard all day. He came home tired and dirty, and was about to go straight to the wash-house to make his toilet when Mr. Green called him in.

"My friend, Mr. Widden," he said, with a satisfied air, as he pointed to a slight, fair young man with a well-trimmed moustache.

Mr. Letts shook hands.

"Fine day," said Mr. Widden.

"Beautiful," said the other. "I'll come in and have a talk about it when I've had a wash."

"Me and Miss Foster are going out for a bit of a stroll," said Mr. Widden.

"Quite right," agreed Mr. Letts. "Much more healthy than staying indoors all the evening. If you just wait while I have a wash and a bit o' something to eat I'll come with you."

"Co-come with us!" said Mr. Widden, after an astonished pause.

Mr. Letts nodded. "You see, I don't know you yet," he explained, "and as head of the family I want to see how you behave yourself. Properly speaking, my consent ought to have been asked before you walked out with her; still, as everybody thought I was drowned, I'll say no more about it."

"Mr. Green knows all about me," said Mr. Widden, rebelliously.

"It's nothing to do with him," declared Mr. Letts. "And, besides, he's not what I should call a judge of character. I dare say you are all right, but I'm going to see for myself. You go on in the ordinary way with your love-making, without taking any notice of me. Try and forget I'm watching you. Be as natural as you can be, and if you do anything I don't like I'll soon tell you of it."

The bewildered Mr. Widden turned, but, reading no hope of assistance in the infuriated eyes of Mr. Green, appealed in despair to Betty.

"I don't mind," she said. "Why should I?"

Mr. Widden could have supplied her with many reasons, but he refrained, and sat in sulky silence while Mr. Letts got ready. From his point of view the experiment was by no means a success, his efforts to be natural being met with amazed glances from Mr. Letts and disdainful requests from Miss Foster to go home if he couldn't behave himself. When he relapsed into moody silence Mr. Letts cleared his throat and spoke.

"There's no need to be like a monkey-on-a-stick, and at the same time there's no need to be sulky," he pointed out; "there's a happy medium."

"Like you, I s'pose?" said the frantic suitor. "Like me," said the other, gravely. "Now, you watch; fall in behind and watch."

He drew Miss Foster's arm through his and, leaning towards her with tender deference, began a long conversation. At the end of ten minutes Mr. Widden intimated that he thought he had learned enough to go on with.

"Ah! that's only your conceit," said Mr. Letts over his shoulder. "I was afraid you was conceited."

He turned to Miss Foster again, and Mr. Widden, with a despairing gesture, abandoned himself to gloom. He made no further interruptions, but at the conclusion of the walk hesitated so long on the door-step that Mr. Letts had to take the initiative.

"Good-night," he said, shaking hands. "Come round to-morrow night and I'll give you another lesson. You're a slow learner, that's what you are; a slow learner."

He gave Mr. Widden a lesson on the following evening, but cautioned him sternly against imitating the display of brotherly fondness of which, in a secluded lane, he had been a wide-eyed observer.

"When you've known her as long as I have—nineteen years," said Mr. Letts, as the other protested, "things'll be a bit different. I might not be here, for one thing."

By exercise of great self-control Mr. Widden checked the obvious retort and walked doggedly in the rear of Miss Foster. Then, hardly able to believe his ears, he heard her say something to Mr. Letts.

"Eh?" said that gentleman, in amazed accents.

"You fall behind," said Miss Foster.

"That—that's not the way to talk to the head of the family," said Mr. Letts, feebly.

"It's the way I talk to him," rejoined the girl.

It was a position for which Mr. Letts was totally unprepared, and the satisfied smile of Mr. Widden as he took the vacant place by no means improved matters. In a state of considerable dismay Mr. Letts dropped farther and farther behind until, looking up, he saw Miss Foster, attended by her restive escort, quietly waiting for him. An odd look in her eyes as they met his gave him food for thought for the rest of the evening.

At the end of what Mr. Letts was pleased to term a month's trial, Mr. Widden was still unable to satisfy him as to his fitness for the position of brother-in-law. In a spirit of gloom he made suggestions of a mutinous nature to Mr. Green, but that gentleman, who had returned one day pale and furious, but tamed, from an interview that related to his treatment of his wife, held out no hopes of assistance.

"I wash my hands of him," he said bitterly. "You stick to it; that's all you can do."

"They lost me last night," said the unfortunate. "I stayed behind just to take a stone out of my shoe, and the earth seemed to swallow them up. He's so strong. That's the worst of it."

"Strong?" said Mr. Green.

Mr. Widden nodded. "Tuesday evening he showed her how he upset a man once and stood him on his head," he said, irritably. "I was what he showed her with."

"Stick to it!" counselled Mr. Green again. "A brother and sister are bound to get tired of each other before long; it's nature."

Mr. Widden sighed and obeyed. But brother and sister showed no signs of tiring of each other's company, while they displayed unmistakable signs of weariness with his. And three weeks later Mr. Letts, in a few well-chosen words, kindly but firmly dismissed him.

"I should never give my consent," he said, gravely, "so it's only wasting your time. You run off and play."

Mr. Widden ran off to Mr. Green, but before he could get a word out discovered that something unusual had happened. Mrs. Green, a picture of distress, sat at one end of the room with a handkerchief to her eyes; Mr. Green, in a condition compounded of joy and rage, was striding violently up and down the room.

"He's a fraud!" he shouted. "A fraud! I've had my suspicions for some time, and this evening I got it out of her."

Mr. Widden stared in amazement.

"I got it out of her," repeated Mr. Green, pointing at the trembling woman. "He's no more her son than what you are."

"What?" said the amazed listener.

"She's been deceiving me," said Mr. Green, with a scowl, "but I don't think she'll do it again in a hurry. You stay here," he shouted, as his wife rose to leave the room. "I want you to be here when he comes in."

Mrs. Green stayed, and the other two, heedless of her presence, discussed the situation until the front door was heard to open, and Mr. Letts and Betty came into the room. With a little cry the girl ran to her mother.

"What's the matter?" she cried.

"She's lost another son," said Mr. Green, with a ferocious sneer—"a flash, bullying, ugly chap of the name o' Letts."

"Halloa!" said Mr. Letts, starting.

"A chap she picked up out of the street, and tried to pass off on me as her son," continued Mr. Green, raising his voice. "She ain't heard the end of it yet, I can tell you."

Mr. Letts fidgeted. "You leave her alone," he said, mildly. "It's true I'm not her son, but it don't matter, because I've been to see a lawyer about her, and he told me that this house and half the furniture belongs by law to Betty. It's got nothing to do with you."

"Indeed!" said Mr. Green. "Now you take yourself off before I put the police on to you. Take your face off these premises."

Mr. Letts, scratching his head, looked vaguely round the room.

"Go on!" vociferated Mr. Green. "Or will you have the police to put you out?"

Mr. Letts cleared his throat and moved towards the door. "You stick up for your rights, my girl," he said, turning to Betty. "If he don't treat your mother well, give him back his kitchen chair and his three stair-rods and pack him off."

"Henry," said Mr. Green, with dangerous calm, "go and fetch a policeman."

"I'm going," said Mr. Letts, hastily. "Good-by, Betty; good-by, mother. I sha'n't be long. I'm only going as far as the post-office. And that reminds me. I've been talking so much that I quite forget to tell you that Betty and me were married yesterday morning."

He nodded pleasantly at the stupefied Mr. Green, and, turning to Mr. Widden, gave him a friendly dig in the ribs with his finger.

"What's mine is Betty's," he said, in a clear voice, "and what's Betty's is MINE! D'ye understand, step-father?"

He stepped over to Mrs. Green, and putting a strong arm around her raised her to her feet. "And what's mine is mother's," he concluded, and, helping her across the room, placed her in the best arm-chair.

Mr. Wragg sat in a high-backed Windsor chair at the door of his house, smoking. Before him the road descended steeply to the harbor, a small blue patch of which was visible from his door. Children over five were at school: children under that age, and suspiciously large for their years, played about in careless disregard of the remarks which Mr. Wragg occasionally launched at them. Twice a ball had whizzed past him; and a small but select party, with a tip-cat of huge dimensions and awesome points, played just out of reach. Mr. Wragg, snapping his eyes nervously, threatened in vain.

"Morning, old crusty-patch," said a cheerful voice at his elbow.

Mr. Wragg glanced up at the young fisherman towering above him, and eyed him disdainfully.

"Why don't you leave 'em alone?" inquired the young man. "Be cheerful and smile at 'em. You'd soon be able to smile with a little practice." "You mind your business, George Gale, and I'll mind mine," said Mr. Wragg, fiercely; "I've 'ad enough of your impudence, and I'm not going to have any more. And don't lean up agin my house, 'cos I won't 'ave it."

Mr. Gale laughed. "Got out o' bed the wrong side again, haven't you?" he inquired. "Why don't you put that side up against the wall?"

Mr. Wragg puffed on in silence and became absorbed in a fishing-boat gliding past at the bottom of the hill.

"I hear you've got a niece coming to live with you?" pursued the young man.

Mr. Wragg smoked on.

"Poor thing!" said the other, with a sigh. "Does she take after you—in looks, I mean?"

"If I was twenty years younger nor what I am," said Mr. Wragg, sententiously, "I'd give you a hiding, George Gale."

"It's what I want," agreed Mr. Gale, placidly. "Well, so long, Mr. Wragg. I can't stand talking to you all day."

He was about to move off, after pretending to pinch the ear of the infuriated Mr. Wragg, when he noticed a station-fly, with a big trunk on the box-seat, crawling slowly up the hill towards them.

"Good riddance," said Mr. Wragg, suggestively.

The other paid no heed. The vehicle came nearer, and a girl, who plainly owed none of her looks to Mr. Wragg's side of the family, came into view behind the trunk. She waved her hand, and Mr. Wragg, removing his pipe from his mouth, waved it in return. Mr. Gale edged away about eighteen inches, and, with an air of assumed carelessness, gazed idly about him.

He saluted the driver as the fly stopped and gazed hard at the apparition that descended. Then he caught his breath as the girl, approaching her uncle, kissed him affectionately. Mr. Wragg, looking up fiercely at Mr. Gale, was surprised at the expression on that gentleman's face.

"Isn't it lovely here?" said the girl, looking about her; "and isn't the air nice?"

She followed Mr. Wragg inside, and the driver, a small man and elderly, began tugging at the huge trunk. Mr. Gale's moment had arrived.

"Stand away, Joe," he said, stepping forward. "I'll take that in for you."

He hoisted the trunk on his shoulders, and, rather glad of his lowered face, advanced slowly into the house. Uncle and niece had just vanished at the head of the stairs, and Mr. Gale, after a moment's hesitation, followed.

"In 'ere," said Mr. Wragg, throwing open a door.

"Halloa! What are you doing in my house? Put it down. Put it down at once; d'ye hear?"

Mr. Gale caught the girl's surprised glance and, somewhat flustered, swung round so suddenly that the corner of the trunk took the gesticulating Mr. Wragg by the side of the head and bumped it against the wall. Deaf to his outcries, Mr. Gale entered the room and placed the box on the floor.

"Where shall I put it?" he inquired of the girl, respectfully.

"You go out of my house," stormed Mr. Wragg, entering with his hand to his head. "Go on. Out you go."

The young man surveyed him with solicitude. "I'm very sorry if I hurt you, Mr. Wragg—" he began.

"Out you go," repeated the other.

"It was a pure accident," pleaded Mr. Gale.

"And don't you set foot in my 'ouse agin," said the vengeful Mr. Wragg. "You made yourself officious bringing that box in a-purpose to give me a clump o' the side of the head with it."

Mr. Gale denied the charge so eagerly, and withal so politely, that the elder man regarded him in amazement. Then his glance fell on his niece, and he smiled with sudden malice as Mr. Gale slowly and humbly descended the stairs.

"One o' the worst chaps about here, my dear," he said, loudly. "Mate o' one o' the fishing-boats, and as impudent as they make 'em. Many's the time I've clouted his head for 'im."

The girl regarded his small figure with surprised respect.

"When he was a boy, I mean," continued Mr. Wragg. "Now, there's your room, and when you've put things to rights, come down and I'll show you over the house."

He glanced at his niece several times during the day, trying hard to trace a likeness, first to his dead sister and then to himself. Several times he scrutinized himself in the small glass on the mantelpiece, but in vain. Even when he twisted his thin beard in his hand and tried to ignore his mustache, the likeness still eluded him.

His opinion of Miss Miller's looks was more than shared by the young men of Waterside. It was a busy youth who could not spare five minutes to chat with an uncle so fortunate, and in less than a couple of weeks Mr. Wragg was astonished at his popularity, and the deference accorded to his opinions.

The most humble of them all was Mr. Gale, and, with a pertinacity which was almost proof against insult, he strove to force his company upon the indignant Mr. Wragg. Debarred from that, he took to haunting the road, on one occasion passing the house no fewer than fifty-seven times in one afternoon. His infatuation was plain to be seen of all men. Wise men closed their eyes to it; others had theirs closed for them, Mr. Gale being naturally incensed to think that there was anything in his behavior that attracted attention.

His father was at sea, and, to the dismay of the old woman who kept house for him, he began to neglect his food. A melancholy but not unpleasing idea that he was slowly fading occurred to him when he found that he could eat only two herrings for breakfast instead of four. His particular friend, Joe Harris, to whom he confided the fact, remonstrated hotly.

"There's plenty of other girls," he suggested.

"Not like her," said Mr. Gale.

"You're getting to be a by-word in the place," complained his friend.

Mr. Gale flushed. "I'd do more than that for her sake," he said, softly.

"It ain't the way," said Mr. Harris, impatiently. "Girls like a man o' spirit; not a chap who hangs about without speaking, and looks as though he has been caught stealing the cat's milk. Why don't you go round and see her one afternoon when old Wragg is out?"

Mr. Gale shivered. "I dursen't," he confessed.

Mr. Harris pondered. "She was going to be a hospital nurse afore she came down here," he said, slowly. "P'r'aps if you was to break your leg or something she'd come and nurse you. She's wonderful fond of it, I understand."

"But then, you see, I haven't broken it," said the other, impatiently.

"You've got a bicycle," said Mr. Harris. "You—wait a minute—" he half-closed his eyes and waved aside a remark of his friend's. "Suppose you 'ad an accident and fell off it, just in front of the house?"

"I never fall off," said Mr. Gale, simply.

"Old Wragg is out, and me and Charlie Brown carry you into the house," continued Mr. Harris, closing his eyes entirely. "When you come to your senses, she's bending over you and crying."

He opened his eyes suddenly and then, closing one, gazed hard at the bewildered Gale. "To-morrow afternoon at two," he said, briskly, "me and Charlie'll be there waiting."

"Suppose old Wragg ain't out?" objected Mr. Gale, after ten minutes' explanation.

"He's at the 'Lobster Pot' five days out of six at that time," was the reply; "if he ain't there tomorrow, it can't be helped."

Mr. Gale spent the evening practising falls in a quiet lane, and by the time night came had attained to such proficiency that on the way home he fell off without intending it. It seemed an easier thing than he had imagined, and next day at two o'clock punctually he put his lessons into practice.

By a slight error in judgment his head came into contact with Mr. Wragg's doorstep, and, half-stunned, he was about to rise, when Mr. Harris rushed up and forced him down again. Mr. Brown, who was also in attendance, helped to restore his faculties by a well-placed kick.

"He's lost his senses," said Mr. Harris, looking up at Miss Miller, as she came to the door.

"You could ha' heard him fall arf a mile away," added Mr. Brown.

Miss Miller stooped and examined the victim carefully. There was a nasty cut on the side of his head, and a general limpness of body which was alarming. She went indoors for some water, and by the time she returned the enterprising Mr. Harris had got the patient in the passage.

"I'm afraid he's going," he said, in answer to the girl's glance.

"Run for the doctor," she said, hastily. "Quick!"

"We don't like to leave 'im, miss," said Mr. Harris, tenderly. "I s'pose it would be too much to ask you to go?"

Miss Miller, with a parting glance at the prostrate man, departed at once.

"What did you do that for?" demanded Mr. Gale, sitting up. "I don't want the doctor; he'll spoil everything. Why didn't you go away and leave us?"

"I sent 'er for the doctor," said Mr. Harris, slowly. "I sent 'er for the doctor so as we can get you to bed afore she comes back."

"Bed?" exclaimed Mr. Gale.

"Up you go," said Mr. Harris, briefly. "We'll tell her we carried you up. Now, don't waste time."

Pushed by his friends, and stopping to expostulate at every step, Mr. Gale was thrust at last into Mr. Wragg's bedroom.

"Off with your clothes," said the leading spirit. "What's the matter with you, Charlie Brown?"

"Don't mind me; I'll be all right in a minute," said that gentleman, wiping his eyes. "I'm thinking of old Wragg."

Before Mr. Gale had made up his mind his coat and waistcoat were off, and Mr. Brown was at work on his boots. In five minutes' time he was tucked up in Mr. Wragg's bed; his clothes were in a neat little pile on a chair, and Messrs. Harris and Brown were indulging in a congratulatory double-shuffle by the window.

"Don't come to your senses yet awhile," said the former; "and when you do, tell the doctor you can't move your limbs."

"If they try to pull you out o' bed," said Mr. Brown, "scream as though you're being killed. H'sh! Here they are."

Voices sounded below; Miss Miller and the doctor had met at the door with Mr. Wragg, and a violent outburst on that gentleman's part died away as he saw that the intruders had disappeared. He was still grumbling when Mr. Harris, putting his head over the balusters, asked him to make a little less noise.

Mr. Wragg came upstairs in three bounds, and his mien was so terrible that Messrs. Harris and Brown huddled together for protection. Then his gaze fell on the bed and he strove in vain for speech.

"We done it for the best," faltered Mr. Harris.

Mr. Wragg made a gurgling noise in his throat, and, as the doctor entered the room, pointed with a trembling finger at the bed. The other two gentlemen edged toward the door.

"Take him away; take him away at once," vociferated Mr. Wragg.

The doctor motioned him to silence, and Joe Harris and Mr. Brown held their breaths nervously as he made an examination. For ten minutes he prodded and puzzled over the insensible form in the bed; then he turned to the couple at the door.

"How did it happen?" he inquired.

Mr. Harris told him. He also added that he thought it was best to put him to bed at once before he came round.

"Quite right," said the doctor, nodding. "It's a very serious case."

"Well, I can't 'ave him 'ere," broke in Mr. Wragg.

"It won't be for long," said the doctor, shaking his head.

"I can't 'ave him 'ere at all, and, what's more, I won't. Let him go to his own bed," said Mr. Wragg, quivering with excitement.

"He is not to be moved," said the doctor, decidedly. "If he comes to his senses and gets out of bed you must coax him back again."

"Coax?" stuttered Mr. Wragg. "Coax? What's he got to do with me? This house isn't a 'orsepittle. Put his clothes on and take 'im away."

"Do nothing of the kind," was the stern reply. "In fact, his clothes had better be taken out of the room, in case he comes round and tries to dress."

Mr. Harris skipped across to the clothes and tucked them gleefully under his arm; Mr. Brown secured the boots.

"When he will come out of this stupor I can't say," continued the doctor. "Keep him perfectly quiet and don't let him see a soul."

"Look 'ere—" began Mr. Wragg, in a broken voice.

"As to diet—water," said the doctor, looking round.

"Water?" said Miss Miller, who had come quietly into the room.

"Water," repeated the doctor; "as much as he likes to take, of course. Let me see: to-day is Tuesday. I'll look in on Friday, or Saturday at latest; but till then he must have nothing but clear cold water."

Mr. Harris shot a horrified glance at the bed, which happened just then to creak. "But s'pose he asks for food, sir?" he said, respectfully.

"He mustn't have it," said the other, sharply. "If he is very insistent," he added, turning to the sullen Mr. Wragg, "tell him that he has just had food. He won't know any better, and he will be quite satisfied."

He motioned them out of the room, and then, lowering the blinds, followed downstairs on tiptoe. A murmur of voices, followed by the closing of the front door, sounded from below; and Mr. Gale, getting cautiously out of bed, saw Messrs. Harris and Brown walk up the street talking earnestly. He stole back on tiptoe to the door, and strove in vain to catch the purport of the low-voiced discussion below. Mr. Wragg's voice was raised, but indistinct. Then he fancied that he heard a laugh.

He waited until the door closed behind the doctor, and then went back to bed, to try and think out a situation which was fast becoming mysterious.

He lay in the darkened room until a cheerful clatter of crockery below heralded the approach of tea-time. He heard Miss Miller call her uncle in from the garden, and with some satisfaction heard her pleasant voice engaged in brisk talk. At intervals Mr. Wragg laughed loud and long.

Tea was cleared away, and the long evening dragged along in silence. Uncle and niece were apparently sitting in the garden, but they came in to supper, and later on the fumes of Mr. Wragg's pipe pervaded the house. At ten o'clock he heard footsteps ascending the stairs, and through half-closed eyes saw Mr. Wragg enter the bedroom with a candle.

"Time the pore feller had 'is water," he said to his niece, who remained outside.

"Unless he is still insensible," was the reply.

Mr. Gale, who was feeling both thirsty and hungry, slowly opened his eyes, and fixed them in a vacant stare on Mr. Wragg.

"Where am I?" he inquired, in a faint voice.

"Buckingham Pallis," replied Mr. Wragg, promptly.

Mr. Gale ground his teeth. "How did I come here?" he said, at last.

"The fairies brought you," said Mr. Wragg.

The young man rubbed his eyes and blinked at the candle. "I seem to remember falling," he said, slowly; "has anything happened?"

"One o' the fairies dropped you," said Mr. Wragg, with great readiness; "fortunately, you fell on your head."

A sound suspiciously like a giggle came from the landing and fell heavily on Gale's ears. He closed his eyes and tried to think.

"How did I get into your bedroom, Mr. Wragg?" he inquired, after a long pause.

"Light-'eaded," confided Mr. Wragg to the landing, and significantly tapping his forehead.

"This ain't my bedroom," he said, turning to the invalid. "It's the King's. His Majesty gave up 'is bed at once, direckly he 'eard you was 'urt."

"And he's going to sleep on three chairs in the front parlor—if he can," said a low voice from the landing.

The humor faded from Mr. Wragg's face and was succeeded by an expression of great sourness. "Where is the pore feller's supper?" he inquired. "I don't suppose he can eat anything, but he might try."

He went to the door and a low-voiced colloquy ensued. The rival merits of cold chicken versus steak-pie as an invalid diet were discussed at some length. Finally the voice of Miss Miller insisted on chicken, and a glass of port-wine.

"I'll tell 'im it's chicken and port-wine then," said Mr. Wragg, reappearing with a bedroom jug and a tumbler, which he placed on a small table by the bedside.

"Don't let him eat too much, mind," said the voice from the landing, anxiously.

Mr. Wragg said that he would be careful, and addressing Mr. Gale implored him not to overeat himself. The young man stared at him offensively, and, pretty certain now of the true state of affairs, thought only of escape.

"I feel better," he said, slowly. "I think I will go home."

"Yes, yes," said the other, soothingly.

"If you will fetch my clothes," continued Mr. Gale, "I will go now."

"Clothes!" said Mr. Wragg, in an astonished voice. "Why, you didn't 'ave any."

Mr. Gale sat up suddenly in bed and shook his fist at him. "Look here—" he began, in a choking voice.

"The fairies brought you as you was," continued Mr. Wragg, grinning furiously; "and of all the perfect pictures—"

A series of gasping sobs sounded from the landing, the stairs creaked, and a door slammed violently below. In spite of this precaution the sounds of a maiden in dire distress were distinctly audible.

"You give me my clothes," shouted the now furious Mr. Gale, springing out of bed.

Mr. Wragg drew back. "I'll go and fetch 'em," he said, hastily.

He ran lightly downstairs, and the young man, sitting on the edge of the bed, waited. Ten minutes passed, and he heard Mr. Wragg returning, followed by his niece. He slipped back into bed again.

"It's a pore brain again," he heard, in the unctuous tones which Mr. Wragg appeared to keep for this emergency. "It's clothes he wants now; by and by I suppose it'll be something else. Well, the doctor said we'd got to humor him."

"Poor fellow!" sighed Miss Miller, with a break in her voice.

"See 'ow his face'll light up when he sees them," said her uncle.

He pushed the door open, and after surveying the patient with a benevolent smile triumphantly held up a collar and tie for his inspection and threw them on the bed. Then he disappeared hastily and, closing the door, turned the key in the lock.

"If you want any more chicken or anything," he cried through the door, "ring the bell."

The horrified prisoner heard them pass downstairs again, and, after a glass of water, sat down by the window and tried to think. He got up and tried the door, but it opened inwards, and after a severe onslaught the handle came off in his hand. Tired out at last he went to bed again, and slept fitfully until morning.

Mr. Wragg visited him again after breakfast, but with great foresight only put his head in at the door, while Miss Miller remained outside in case of need. In these circumstances Mr. Gale met his anxious inquiries with a sullen silence, and the other, tired at last of baiting him, turned to go.

"I'll be back soon," he said, with a grin. "I'm just going out to tell folks 'ow you're getting on. There's a lot of 'em anxious."

He was as good as his word, and Mr. Gale, peeping from the window, raged helplessly as little knots of neighbors stood smiling up at the house. Unable to endure it any longer he returned to bed, resolving to wait until night came, and then drop from the window and run home in a blanket.

The smell of dinner was almost painful, but he made no sign. Mr. Wragg in high good humor smoked a pipe after his meal, and then went out again. The house was silent except for the occasional movements of the girl below. Then there was a sudden tap at his door.

"Well?" said Mr. Gale.

The door opened and, hardly able to believe his eyes, he saw his clothes thrown into the room. Hunger was forgotten, and he almost smiled as he hastily dressed himself.

The smile vanished as he thought of the people in the streets, and in a thoughtful fashion he made his way slowly downstairs. The bright face of Miss Miller appeared at the parlor door.

"Better?" she smiled.

Mr. Gale reddened and, drawing himself up stiffly, made no reply.

"That's polite," said the girl, indignantly. "After giving you your clothes, too. What do you think my uncle will say to me? He was going to keep you here till Friday."

Mr. Gale muttered an apology. "I've made a fool of myself," he added.

Miss Miller nodded cheerfully. "Are you hungry?" she inquired.

The other drew himself up again.

"Because there is some nice cold beef left," said the girl, glancing into the room.

Mr. Gale started and, hardly able to believe in his good fortune, followed her inside. In a very short time the cold beef was a thing of the past, and the young man, toying with his beer-glass, sat listening to a lecture on his behavior couched in the severest terms his hostess could devise.

"You'll be the laughing-stock of the place," she concluded.

"I shall go away," he said, gloomily.

"I shouldn't do that," said the girl, with a judicial air; "live it down."

"I shall go away," repeated Mr. Gale, decidedly. "I shall ship for a deep-sea voyage."

Miss Miller sighed. "It's too bad," she said, slowly; "perhaps you wouldn't look so foolish if—"

"If what?" inquired the other, after a long pause.

"If," said Miss Miller, looking down, "if—if—"

Mr. Gale started and trembled violently, as a wild idea, born of her blushes, occurred to him.

"If," he said, in quivering tones, "if—if—"

"Go on," said the girl, softly. "Why, I got as far as that: and you are a man."

Mr. Gale's voice became almost inaudible. "If we got married, do you mean?" he said, at last.

"Married!" exclaimed Miss Miller, starting back a full two inches. "Good gracious! the man is mad after all."

The bitter and loudly expressed opinion of Mr. Wragg when he returned an hour later was that they were both mad.

Farmer Rose sat in his porch smoking an evening pipe. By his side, in a comfortable Windsor chair, sat his friend the miller, also smoking, and gazing with half-closed eyes at the landscape as he listened for the thousandth time to his host's complaints about his daughter.

"The long and the short of it is, Cray," said the farmer, with an air of mournful pride, "she's far too good-looking."

Mr. Cray grunted.

"Truth is truth, though she's my daughter," continued Mr. Rose, vaguely. "She's too good-looking. Sometimes when I've taken her up to market I've seen the folks fair turn their backs on the cattle and stare at her instead."

Mr. Cray sniffed; louder, perhaps, than he had intended. "Beautiful that rose-bush smells," he remarked, as his friend turned and eyed him.

"What is the consequence?" demanded the farmer, relaxing his gaze. "She looks in the glass and sees herself, and then she gets miserable and uppish because there ain't nobody in these parts good enough for her to marry."

"It's a extraordinary thing to me where she gets them good looks from," said the miller, deliberately.

"Ah!" said Mr. Rose, and sat trying to think of a means of enlightening his friend without undue loss of modesty.

"She ain't a bit like her poor mother," mused Mr. Cray.

"No, she don't get her looks from her," assented the other.

"It's one o' them things you can't account for," said Mr. Cray, who was very tired of the subject; "it's just like seeing a beautiful flower blooming on an old cabbage-stump."

The farmer knocked his pipe out noisily and began to refill it. "People have said that she takes after me a trifle," he remarked, shortly.

"You weren't fool enough to believe that, I know," said the miller. "Why, she's no more like you than you're like a warming-pan—not so much."

Mr. Rose regarded his friend fixedly. "You ain't got a very nice way o' putting things, Cray," he said, mournfully.

"I'm no flatterer," said the miller; "never was. And you can't please everybody. If I said your daughter took after you I don't s'pose she'd ever speak to me again."

"The worst of it is," said the farmer, disregarding his remark, "she won't settle down. There's young Walter Lomas after her now, and she won't look at him. He's a decent young fellow is Walter, and she's been and named one o' the pigs after him, and the way she mixes them up together is disgraceful."

"If she was my girl she should marry young Walter," said the miller, firmly. "What's wrong with him?"

"She looks higher," replied the other, mysteriously; "she's always reading them romantic books full o' love tales, and she's never tired o' talking of a girl her mother used to know that went on the stage and married a baronet. She goes and sits in the best parlor every afternoon now, and calls it the drawing-room. She'll sit there till she's past the marrying age, and then she'll turn round and blame me."

"She wants a lesson," said Mr. Cray, firmly. "She wants to be taught her position in life, not to go about turning up her nose at young men and naming pigs after them."

Mr. Rose sighed.

"What she wants to understand is that the upper classes wouldn't look at her," pursued the miller.

"It would be easier to make her understand that if they didn't," said the farmer.

"I mean," said Mr. Cray, sternly, "with a view to marriage. What you ought to do is to get somebody staying down here with you pretending to be a lord or a nobleman, and ordering her about and not noticing her good looks at all. Then, while she's upset about that, in comes Walter Lomas to comfort her and be a contrast to the other."

Mr. Rose withdrew his pipe and regarded him open-mouthed.

"Yes; but how—" he began.

"And it seems to me," interrupted Mr. Cray, "that I know just the young fellow to do it—nephew of my wife's. He was coming to stay a fortnight with us, but you can have him with pleasure—me and him don't get on over and above well."

"Perhaps he wouldn't do it," objected the farmer.

"He'd do it like a shot," said Mr. Cray, positively. "It would be fun for us and it 'ud be a lesson for her. If you like, I'll tell him to write to you for lodgings, as he wants to come for a fortnight's fresh air after the fatiguing gayeties of town."

"Fatiguing gayeties of town," repeated the admiring farmer. "Fatiguing—"

He sat back in his chair and laughed, and Mr. Cray, delighted at the prospect of getting rid so easily of a tiresome guest, laughed too. Overhead at the open window a third person laughed, but in so quiet and well-bred a fashion that neither of them heard her.

The farmer received a letter a day or two afterwards, and negotiations between Jane Rose on the one side and Lord Fairmount on the other were soon in progress; the farmer's own composition being deemed somewhat crude for such a correspondence.

"I wish he didn't want it kept so secret," said Miss Rose, pondering over the final letter. "I should like to let the Grays and one or two more people know he is staying with us. However, I suppose he must have his own way."

"You must do as he wishes," said her father, using his handkerchief violently.

Jane sighed. "He'll be a little company for me, at any rate," she remarked. "What is the matter, father?"

"Bit of a cold," said the farmer, indistinctly, as he made for the door, still holding his handkerchief to his face. "Been coming on some time."

He put on his hat and went out, and Miss Rose, watching him from the window, was not without fears that the joke might prove too much for a man of his habit. She regarded him thoughtfully, and when he returned at one o'clock to dinner, and encountered instead a violent dust-storm which was raging in the house, she noted with pleasure that his sense of humor was more under control.

"Dinner?" she said, as he strove to squeeze past the furniture which was piled in the hall. "We've got no time to think of dinner, and if we had there's no place for you to eat it. You'd better go in the larder and cut yourself a crust of bread and cheese."

Her father hesitated and glared at the servant, who, with her head bound up in a duster, passed at the double with a broom. Then he walked slowly into the kitchen.

Miss Rose called out something after him.

"Eh?" said her father, coming back hopefully.

"How is your cold, dear?"

The farmer made no reply, and his daughter smiled contentedly as she heard him stamping about in the larder. He made but a poor meal, and then, refusing point-blank to assist Annie in moving the piano, went and smoked a very reflective pipe in the garden.

Lord Fairmount arrived the following day on foot from the station, and after acknowledging the farmer's salute with a distant nod requested him to send a cart for his luggage. He was a tall, good-looking young man, and as he stood in the hall languidly twisting his mustache Miss Rose deliberately decided upon his destruction.

"These your daughters?" he inquired, carelessly, as he followed his host into the parlor.

"One of 'em is, my lord; the other is my servant," replied the farmer.

"She's got your eyes," said his lordship, tapping the astonished Annie under the chin; "your nose too, I think."

"That's my servant," said the farmer, knitting his brows at him.

"Oh, indeed!" said his lordship, airily.

He turned round and regarded Jane, but, although she tried to meet him half-way by elevating her chin a little, his audacity failed him and the words died away on his tongue. A long silence followed, broken only by the ill-suppressed giggles of Annie, who had retired to the kitchen.

"I trust that we shall make your lordship comfortable," said Miss Rose.

"I hope so, my good girl," was the reply. "And now will you show me my room?"

Miss Rose led the way upstairs and threw open the door; Lord Fairmount, pausing on the threshold, gazed at it disparagingly.

"Is this the best room you have?" he inquired, stiffly.

"Oh, no," said Miss Rose, smiling; "father's room is much better than this. Look here."

She threw open another door and, ignoring a gesticulating figure which stood in the hall below, regarded him anxiously. "If you would prefer father's room he would be delighted for you to have it. Delighted."

"Yes, I will have this one," said Lord Fairmount, entering. "Bring me up some hot water, please, and clear these boots and leggings out."

Miss Rose tripped downstairs and, bestowing a witching smile upon her sire, waved away his request for an explanation and hastened into the kitchen, whence Annie shortly afterwards emerged with the water.

It was with something of a shock that the farmer discovered that he had to wait for his dinner while his lordship had luncheon. That meal, under his daughter's management, took a long time, and the joint when it reached him was more than half cold. It was, moreover, quite clear that the aristocracy had not even mastered the rudiments of carving, but preferred instead to box the compass for tit-bits.

He ate his meal in silence, and when it was over sought out his guest to administer a few much-needed stage-directions. Owing, however, to the ubiquity of Jane he wasted nearly the whole of the afternoon before he obtained an opportunity. Even then the interview was short, the farmer having to compress into ten seconds instructions for Lord Fairmount to express a desire to take his meals with the family, and his dinner at the respectable hour of 1 p.m. Instructions as to a change of bedroom were frustrated by the reappearance of Jane.

His lordship went for a walk after that, and coming back with a bored air stood on the hearthrug in the living-room and watched Miss Rose sewing.

"Very dull place," he said at last, in a dissatisfied voice.

"Yes, my lord," said Miss Rose, demurely.

"Fearfully dull," complained his lordship, stifling a yawn. "What I'm to do to amuse myself for a fortnight I'm sure I don't know."

Miss Rose raised her fine eyes and regarded him intently. Many a lesser man would have looked no farther for amusement.

"I'm afraid there is not much to do about here, my lord," she said quietly. "We are very plain folk in these parts."

"Yes," assented the other. An obvious compliment rose of itself to his lips, but he restrained himself, though with difficulty. Miss Rose bent her head over her work and stitched industriously. His lordship took up a book and, remembering his mission, read for a couple of hours without taking the slightest notice of her. Miss Rose glanced over in his direction once or twice, and then, with a somewhat vixenish expression on her delicate features, resumed her sewing.

"Wonderful eyes she's got," said the gentleman, as he sat on the edge of his bed that night and thought over the events of the day. "It's pretty to see them flash."

He saw them flash several times during the next few days, and Mr. Rose himself, was more than satisfied with the hauteur with which his guest treated the household.

"But I don't like the way you have with me," he complained.

"It's all in the part," urged his lordship.

"Well, you can leave that part out," rejoined Mr. Rose, with some acerbity. "I object to being spoke to as you speak to me before that girl Annie. Be as proud and unpleasant as you like to my daughter, but leave me alone. Mind that!"

His lordship promised, and in pursuance of his host's instructions strove manfully to subdue feelings towards Miss Rose by no means in accordance with them. The best of us are liable to absent-mindedness, and he sometimes so far forgot himself as to address her in tones as humble as any in her somewhat large experience.

"I hope that we are making you comfortable here, my lord?" she said, as they sat together one afternoon.

"I have never been more comfortable in my life," was the gracious reply.

Miss Rose shook her head. "Oh, my lord," she said, in protest, "think of your mansion."

His lordship thought of it. For two or three days he had been thinking of houses and furniture and other things of that nature.

"I have never seen an old country seat," continued Miss Rose, clasping her hands and gazing at him wistfully. "I should be so grateful if your lordship would describe yours to me."

His lordship shifted uneasily, and then, in face of the girl's persistence, stood for some time divided between the contending claims of Hampton Court Palace and the Tower of London. He finally decided upon the former, after first refurnishing it at Maple's.

"How happy you must be!" said the breathless Jane, when he had finished.

He shook his head gravely. "My possessions have never given me any happiness," he remarked. "I would much rather be in a humble rank of life. Live where I like, and—and marry whom I like."

There was no mistaking the meaning fall in his voice. Miss Rose sighed gently and lowered her eyes—her lashes had often excited comment. Then, in a soft voice, she asked him the sort of life he would prefer.

In reply, his lordship, with an eloquence which surprised himself, portrayed the joys of life in a seven-roomed house in town, with a greenhouse six feet by three, and a garden large enough to contain it. He really spoke well, and when he had finished his listener gazed at him with eyes suffused with timid admiration.

"Oh, my lord," she said, prettily, "now I know what you've been doing. You've been slumming."

"Slumming?" gasped his lordship.

"You couldn't have described a place like that unless you had been," said Miss Rose nodding. "I hope you took the poor people some nice hot soup."

His lordship tried to explain, but without success. Miss Rose persisted in regarding him as a missionary of food and warmth, and spoke feelingly of the people who had to live in such places. She also warned him against the risk of infection.

"You don't understand," he repeated, impatiently. "These are nice houses—nice enough for anybody to live in. If you took soup to people like that, why, they'd throw it at you."

"Wretches!" murmured the indignant Jane, who was enjoying herself amazingly.

His lordship eyed her with sudden suspicion, but her face was quite grave and bore traces of strong feeling. He explained again, but without avail.

"You never ought to go near such places, my lord," she concluded, solemnly, as she rose to quit the room. "Even a girl of my station would draw the line at that."

She bowed deeply and withdrew. His lordship sank into a chair and, thrusting his hands into his pockets, gazed gloomily at the dried grasses in the grate.

During the next day or two his appetite failed, and other well-known symptoms set in. Miss Rose, diagnosing them all, prescribed by stealth some bitter remedies. The farmer regarded his change of manner with disapproval, and, concluding that it was due to his own complaints, sought to reassure him. He also pointed out that his daughter's opinion of the aristocracy was hardly likely to increase if the only member she knew went about the house as though he had just lost his grandmother.

"You are longing for the gayeties of town, my lord," he remarked one morning at breakfast.

His lordship shook his head. The gayeties comprised, amongst other things, a stool and a desk.

"I don't like town," he said, with a glance at Jane. "If I had my choice I would live here always. I would sooner live here in this charming spot with this charming society than anywhere."

Mr. Rose coughed and, having caught his eye, shook his head at him and glanced significantly over at the unconscious Jane. The young man ignored his action and, having got an opening, gave utterance in the course of the next ten minutes to Radical heresies of so violent a type that the farmer could hardly keep his seat. Social distinctions were condemned utterly, and the House of Lords referred to as a human dust-bin. The farmer gazed open-mouthed at this snake he had nourished.

"Your lordship will alter your mind when you get to town," said Jane, demurely.

"Never!" declared the other, impressively.

The girl sighed, and gazing first with much interest at her parent, who seemed to be doing his best to ward off a fit, turned her lustrous eyes upon the guest.

"We shall all miss you," she said, softly. "You've been a lesson to all of us."

"Lesson?" he repeated, flushing.

"It has improved our behavior so, having a lord in the house," said Miss Rose, with painful humility. "I'm sure father hasn't been like the same man since you've been here."

"What d'ye mean Miss?" demanded the farmer, hotly.

"Don't speak like that before his lordship, father," said his daughter, hastily. "I'm not blaming you; you're no worse than the other men about here. You haven't had an opportunity of learning before, that's all. It isn't your fault."

"Learning?" bellowed the farmer, turning an inflamed visage upon his apprehensive guest. "Have you noticed anything wrong about my behavior?"

"Certainly not," said his lordship, hastily.

"All I know is," continued Miss Rose, positively, "I wish you were going to stay here another six months for father's sake."

"Look here—" began Mr. Rose, smiting the table.

"And Annie's," said Jane, raising her voice above the din. "I don't know which has improved the most. I'm sure the way they both drink their tea now—"

Mr. Rose pushed his chair back loudly and got up from the table. For a moment he stood struggling for words, then he turned suddenly with a growl and quitted the room, banging the door after him in a fashion which clearly indicated that he still had some lessons to learn.

"You've made your father angry," said his lordship.

"It's for his own good," said Miss Rose. "Are you really sorry to leave us?"

"Sorry?" repeated the other. "Sorry is no word for it."

"You will miss father," said the girl.

He sighed gently.

"And Annie," she continued.

He sighed again, and Jane took a slight glance at him cornerwise.

"And me too, I hope," she said, in a low voice.

"Miss you!" repeated his lordship, in a suffocating voice. "I should miss the sun less."

"I am so glad," said Jane, clasping her hands; "it is so nice to feel that one is not quite forgotten. Of course, I can never forget you. You are the only nobleman I have ever met."

"I hope that it is not only because of that," he said, forlornly.

Miss Rose pondered. When she pondered her eyes increased in size and revealed unsuspected depths.

"No-o," she said at length, in a hesitating voice.

"Suppose that I were not what I am represented to be," he said slowly. "Suppose that, instead of being Lord Fairmount, I were merely a clerk."

"A clerk?" repeated Miss Rose, with a very well-managed shudder. "How can I suppose such an absurd thing as that?"

"But if I were?" urged his lordship, feverishly.

"It's no use supposing such a thing as that," said Miss Rose, briskly; "your high birth is stamped on you."

His lordship shook his head. "I would sooner be a laborer on this farm than a king anywhere else," he said, with feeling.

Miss Rose drew a pattern on the floor with the toe of her shoe.

"The poorest laborer on the farm can have the pleasure of looking at you every day," continued his lordship passionately. "Every day of his life he can see you, and feel a better man for it."

Miss Rose looked at him sharply. Only the day before the poorest laborer had seen her—when he wasn't expecting the honor—and received an epitome of his character which had nearly stunned him. But his lordship's face was quite grave.

"I go to-morrow," he said.

"Yes," said Jane, in a hushed voice.

He crossed the room gently and took a seat by her side. Miss Rose, still gazing at the floor, wondered indignantly why it was she was not blushing. His Lordship's conversation had come to a sudden stop and the silence was most awkward.

"I've been a fool, Miss Rose," he said at last, rising and standing over her; "and I've been taking a great liberty. I've been deceiving you for nearly a fortnight."

"Nonsense!" responded Miss Rose, briskly.

"I have been deceiving you," he repeated. "I have made you believe that I am a person of title."

"Nonsense!" said Miss Rose again.

The other started and eyed her uneasily.

"Nobody would mistake you for a lord," said Miss Rose, cruelly. "Why, I shouldn't think that you had ever seen one. You didn't do it at all properly. Why, your uncle Cray would have done it better." Mr. Cray's nephew fell back in consternation and eyed her dumbly as she laughed. All mirth is not contagious, and he was easily able to refrain from joining in this.

"I can't understand," said Miss Rose, as she wiped a tear-dimmed eye—"I can't understand how you could have thought I should be so stupid."

"I've been a fool," said the other, bitterly, as he retreated to the door. "Good-by."

"Good-by," said Jane. She looked him full in the face, and the blushes for which she had been waiting came in force. "You needn't go, unless you want to," she said, softly. "I like fools better than lords."

HIS OTHER SELF

"They're as like as two peas, him and 'is brother," said the night-watchman, gazing blandly at the indignant face of the lighterman on the barge below; "and the on'y way I know this one is Sam is because Bill don't use bad langwidge. Twins they are, but the likeness is only outside; Bill's 'art is as white as snow."

He cut off a plug of tobacco, and, placing it in his cheek, waited expectantly.

"White as snow," he repeated.

"That's me," said the lighterman, as he pushed his unwieldy craft from the jetty. "I'll tell Sam your opinion of 'im. So long."

The watchman went a shade redder than usual. That's twins all over, he said, sourly, always deceiving people. It's Bill arter all, and, instead of hurting 'is feelings, I've just been flattering of 'im up.

It ain't the fust time I've 'ad trouble over a likeness. I've been a twin myself in a manner o' speaking. It didn't last long, but it lasted long enough for me to always be sorry for twins, and to make a lot of allowance for them. It must be very 'ard to have another man going about with your face on 'is shoulders, and getting it into trouble.

It was a year or two ago now. I was sitting one evening at the gate, smoking a pipe and looking at a newspaper I 'ad found in the office, when I see a gentleman coming along from the swing-bridge. Well-dressed, clean-shaved chap 'e was, smoking a cigarette. He was walking slow and looking about 'im casual-like, until his eyes fell on me, when he gave a perfect jump of surprise, and, arter looking at me very 'ard, walked on a little way and then turned back. He did it twice, and I was just going to say something to 'im, something that I 'ad been getting ready for 'im, when he spoke to me.

"Good evening," he ses.

"Good evening," I ses, folding the paper over and looking at 'im rather severe.

"I hope you'll excuse me staring," he ses, very perlite; "but I've never seen such a face and figger as yours in all my life—never."

"Ah, you ought to ha' seen me a few years ago," I ses. "I'm like everybody else—I'm getting on."

"Rubbish!" he ses. "You couldn't be better if you tried. It's marvellous! Wonderful! It's the very thing I've been looking for. Why, if you'd been made to order you couldn't ha' been better."

I thought at fust he was by way of trying to get a drink out o' me—I've been played that game afore—but instead o' that he asked me whether I'd do 'im the pleasure of 'aving one with 'im.

We went over to the Albion, and I believe I could have 'ad it in a pail if I'd on'y liked to say the word. And all the time I was drinking he was looking me up and down, till I didn't know where to look, as the saying is.

"I came down 'ere to look for somebody like you," he ses, "but I never dreamt I should have such luck as this. I'm an actor, and I've got to play the part of a sailor, and I've been worried some time 'ow to make up for the part. D'ye understand?"

"No," I ses, looking at 'im.

"I want to look the real thing," he ses, speaking low so the landlord shouldn't hear. "I want to make myself the living image of you. If that don't fetch 'em I'll give up the stage and grow cabbages."

"Make yourself like me?" I ses. "Why, you're no more like me than I'm like a sea-sick monkey."

"Not so much," he ses. "That's where the art comes in."

He stood me another drink, and then, taking my arm in a cuddling sort o' way, and calling me "Dear boy," 'e led me back to the wharf and explained. He said 'e would come round next evening with wot 'e called his make-up box, and paint 'is face and make 'imself up till people wouldn't know one from the other.

"And wot about your figger?" I ses, looking at 'im.

"A cushion," he ses, winking, "or maybe a couple. And what about clothes? You'll 'ave to sell me those you've got on. Hat and all. And boots."

I put a price on 'em that I thought would 'ave finished 'im then and there, but it didn't. And at last, arter paying me so many more compliments that they began to get into my 'ead, he fixed up a meeting for the next night and went off.

"And mind," he ses, coming back, "not a word to a living soul!"

He went off agin, and, arter going to the Bull's Head and 'aving a pint to clear my 'ead, I went and sat down in the office and thought it over. It seemed all right to me as far as I could see; but p'r'aps the pint didn't clear my 'ead enough—p'r'aps I ought to 'ave 'ad two pints.

I lay awake best part of next day thinking it over, and when I got up I 'ad made up my mind. I put my clothes in a sack, and then I put on some others as much like 'em as possible, on'y p'r'aps a bit older, in case the missis should get asking questions; and then I sat wondering 'ow to get out with the sack without 'er noticing it. She's got a very inquiring mind, and I wasn't going to tell her any lies about it. Besides which I couldn't think of one.

I got out at last by playing a game on her. I pertended to drop 'arf a dollar in the washus, and while she was busy on 'er hands and knees I went off as comfortable as you please.

I got into the office with it all right, and, just as it was getting dark, a cab drove up to the wharf and the actor-chap jumped out with a big leather bag. I took 'im into the private office, and 'e was so ready with 'is money for the clothes that I offered to throw the sack in.

He changed into my clothes fust of all, and then, asking me to sit down in front of 'im, he took a looking-glass and a box out of 'is bag and began to alter 'is face. Wot with sticks of coloured paint, and false eyebrows, and a beard stuck on with gum and trimmed with a pair o' scissors, it was more like a conjuring trick than anything else. Then 'e took a wig out of 'is bag and pressed it on his 'ead, put on the cap, put some black stuff on 'is teeth, and there he was. We both looked into the glass together while 'e gave the finishing touches, and then he clapped me on the back and said I was the handsomest sailorman in England.

"I shall have to make up a bit 'eavier when I'm behind the floats," he ses; "but this is enough for 'ere. Wot do you think of the imitation of your voice? I think I've got it exact."

"If you ask me," I ses, "it sounds like a poll-parrot with a cold in the 'ead."

"And now for your walk," he ses, looking as pleased as if I'd said something else. "Come to the door and see me go up the wharf."

I didn't like to hurt 'is feelings, but I thought I should ha' bust. He walked up that wharf like a dancing-bear in a pair of trousers too tight for it, but 'e was so pleased with 'imself that I didn't like to tell 'im so. He went up and down two or three times, and I never saw anything so ridikerlous in my life.

"That's all very well for us," he ses; "but wot about other people? That's wot I want to know. I'll go and 'ave a drink, and see whether anybody spots me."

Afore I could stop 'im he started off to the Bull's Head and went in, while I stood outside and watched 'im.

"'Arf a pint o' four ale," he ses, smacking down a penny.

I see the landlord draw the beer and give it to 'im, but 'e didn't seem to take no notice of 'im. Then, just to open 'is eyes a bit, I walked in and put down a penny and asked for a 'arf-pint.

The landlord was just wiping down the counter at the time, and when I gave my order he looked up and stood staring at me with the wet cloth 'eld up in the air. He didn't say a word—not a single word. He stood there for a moment smiling at us foolish-like, and then 'e let go o' the beer-injin, wot 'e was 'olding in 'is left hand, and sat down heavy on the bar floor. We both put our 'eads over the counter to see wot had 'appened to 'im, and 'e started making the most 'orrible noise I 'ave ever heard in my life. I wonder it didn't bring the fire-injins. The actor-chap bolted out as if he'd been shot, and I was just thinking of follering 'im when the landlord's wife and 'is two daughters came rushing out and asking me wot I 'ad done to him.

"There—there—was two of 'im !" ses the landlord, trembling and holding on to 'is wife's arm, as they helped 'im up and got 'im in the chair. "Two of 'im!"

"Two of wot?" ses his wife.

"Two—two watchmen," ses the landlord; "both exac'ly alike and both asking for 'arf a pint o' four ale."

"Yes, yes," ses 'is wife.

"You come and lay down, pa," ses the gals. "I tell you there was," ses the landlord, getting 'is colour back, with temper.

"Yes, yes; I know all about it," ses 'is wife. "You come inside for a bit; and, Gertie, you bring your father in a soda—a large soda."

They got 'im in arter a lot o' trouble; but three times 'e came back as far as the door, 'olding on to them, and taking a little peep at me. The last time he shook his 'ead at me, and said if I did it agin I could go and get my 'arf-pints somewhere else.

I finished the beer wot the actor 'ad left, and, arter telling the landlord I 'oped his eyesight 'ud be better in the morning, I went outside, and arter a careful look round walked back to the wharf.

I pushed the wicket open a little way and peeped in. The actor was standing just by the fust crane talking to two of the hands off of the Saltram. He'd got 'is back to the light, but 'ow it was they didn't twig his voice I can't think.

They was so busy talking that I crept along by the side of the wall and got to the office without their seeing me. I went into the private office and turned out the gas there, and sat down to wait for 'im. Then I 'eard a noise outside that took me to the door agin and kept me there, 'olding on to the door-post and gasping for my breath. The cook of the Saltram was sitting on a paraffin-cask playing the mouth-orgin, and the actor, with 'is arms folded across his stummick, was dancing a horn-pipe as if he'd gorn mad.

I never saw anything so ridikerlous in my life, and when I recollected that they thought it was me, I thought I should ha' dropped.

A night-watchman can't be too careful, and I knew that it 'ud be all over Wapping next morning that I 'ad been dancing to a tuppenny-ha'penny mouth-orgin played by a ship's cook. A man that does 'is dooty always has a lot of people ready to believe the worst of 'im.

I went back into the dark office and waited, and by and by I 'eard them coming along to the gate and patting 'im on the back and saying he ought to be in a pantermime instead o' wasting 'is time night-watching. He left 'em at the gate, and then 'e came into the office smiling as if he'd done something clever.

"Wot d'ye think of me for a understudy?" he ses, laughing. "They all thought it was you. There wasn't one of 'em 'ad the slightest suspicion —not one."

"And wot about my character?" I ses, folding my arms acrost my chest and looking at him.

"Character?" he ses, staring. "Why, there's no 'arm in dancing; it's a innercent enjoyment."

"It ain't one o' my innercent enjoyments," I ses, "and I don't want to get the credit of it. If they hadn't been sitting in a pub all the evening they'd 'ave spotted you at once."

"Oh!" he ses, very huffy. "How?"

"Your voice," I ses. "You try and mimic a poll-parrot, and think it's like me. And, for another thing, you walk about as though you're stuffed with sawdust."

"I beg your pardon," he ses; "the voice and the walk are exact. Exact."

"Wot?" I ses, looking 'im up and down. "You stand there and 'ave the impudence to tell me that my voice is like that?"

"I do," he ses.

"Then I'm sorry for you," I ses. "I thought you'd got more sense."

He stood looking at me and gnawing 'is finger, and by and by he ses, "Are you married?" he ses.

"I am," I ses, very short.

"Where do you live?" he ses.

I told 'im.

"Very good," he ses; "p'r'aps I'll be able to convince you arter all. By the way, wot do you call your wife? Missis?"

"Yes," I ses, staring at him. "But wot's it got to do with you?"

"Nothing," he ses. "Nothing. Only I'm going to try the poll-parrot voice and the sawdust walk on her, that's all. If I can deceive 'er that'll settle it."

"Deceive her?" I ses. "Do you think I'm going to let you go round to my 'ouse and get me into trouble with the missis like that? Why, you must be crazy; that dancing must 'ave got into your 'ead."

"Where's the 'arm?" he ses, very sulky.

"'*Arm*?" I ses. "I won't 'ave it, that's all; and if you knew my missis you'd know without any telling."

"I'll bet you a pound to a sixpence she wouldn't know me," he ses, very earnest.

"She won't 'ave the chance," I ses, "so that's all about it."

He stood there argufying for about ten minutes; but I was as firm as a rock. I wouldn't move an inch, and at last, arter we was both on the point of losing our tempers, he picked up his bag and said as 'ow he must be getting off 'ome.

"But ain't you going to take those things off fust?" I ses.

"No," he ses, smiling. "I'll wait till I get 'ome. Ta-ta."

He put 'is bag on 'is shoulder and walked to the gate, with me follering of 'im.

"I expect I shall see a cab soon," he ses. "Good-bye."

"Wot are you laughing at?" I ses.

"On'y thoughts," he ses.

"'Ave you got far to go?' I ses.

"No; just about the same distance as you 'ave," he ses, and he went off spluttering like a soda-water bottle.

I took the broom and 'ad a good sweep-up arter he 'ad gorn, and I was just in the middle of it when the cook and the other two chaps from the Saltram came back, with three other sailormen and a brewer's drayman they 'ad brought to see me DANCE!

"Same as you did a little while ago, Bill," ses the cook, taking out 'is beastly mouth-orgin and wiping it on 'is sleeve. "Wot toon would you like?"

I couldn't get away from 'em, and when I told them I 'ad never danced in my life the cook asked me where I expected to go to. He told the drayman that I'd been dancing like a fairy in sea-boots, and they all got in front of me and wouldn't let me pass. I lost my temper at last, and, arter they 'ad taken the broom away from me and the drayman and one o' the sailormen 'ad said wot they'd do to me if I was on'y fifty years younger, they sheered off.

I locked the gate arter 'em and went back to the office, and I 'adn't been there above 'arf an hour when somebody started ringing the gate-bell as if they was mad. I thought it was the cook's lot come back at fust, so I opened the wicket just a trifle and peeped out. There was a 'ansom-cab standing outside, and I 'ad hardly got my nose to the crack when the actor-chap, still in my clothes, pushed the door open and nipped in.

"You've lost," he ses, pushing the door to and smiling all over. "Where's your sixpence?"

"Lost?" I ses, hardly able to speak. "D'ye mean to tell me you've been to my wife arter all—arter all I said to you?"

"I do," he ses, nodding, and smiling agin. "They were both deceived as easy as easy."

"Both?" I ses, staring at 'im. "Both wot? 'Ow many wives d'ye think I've got? Wot d'ye mean by it?"

"Arter I left you," he ses, giving me a little poke in the ribs, "I picked up a cab and, fust leaving my bag at Aldgate, I drove on to your 'ouse and knocked at the door. I knocked twice, and then an angry-looking woman opened it and asked me wot I wanted.

"'It's all right, missis,' I ses. 'I've got 'arf an hour off, and I've come to take you out for a walk.'

"'Wot?' she ses, drawing back with a start.

"'Just a little turn round to see the shops,' I ses; 'and if there's anything particler you'd like and it don't cost too much, you shall 'ave it.'

"I thought at fust, from the way she took it, she wasn't used to you giving 'er things.

"'Ow dare you!' she ses. 'I'll 'ave you locked up. 'Ow dare you insult a respectable married woman! You wait till my 'usband comes 'ome.'

"'But I am your 'usband,' I ses. 'Don't you know me, my pretty? Don't you know your pet sailor-boy?'

"She gave a screech like a steam-injin, and then she went next door and began knocking away like mad. Then I see that I 'ad gorn to number twelve instead of number fourteen. Your wife, your real wife, came out of number fourteen—and she was worse than the other. But they both thought it was you—there's no doubt of that. They chased me all the way up the road, and if it 'adn't ha' been for this cab that was just passing I don't know wot would 'ave 'appened to me."

He shook his 'ead and smiled agin, and, arter opening the wicket a trifle and telling the cabman he shouldn't be long, he turned to me and asked me for the sixpence, to wear on his watch-chain.

"Sixpence!" I ses. "SIXPENCE!" Wot do you think is going to 'appen to me when I go 'ome?"

"Oh, I 'adn't thought o' that," he ses. "Yes, o' course."

"Wot about my wife's jealousy?" I ses. "Wot about the other, and her 'usband, a cooper as big as a 'ouse?"

"Well, well," he ses, "one can't think of everything. It'll be all the same a hundred years hence."

"Look 'ere," I ses, taking 'is shoulder in a grip of iron. "You come back with me now in that cab and explain. D'ye see? That's wot you've got to do."

"All right," he ses; "certainly. Is—is the husband bad-tempered?"

"You'll see," I ses; "but that's your business. Come along."

"With pleasure," he ses, 'elping me in. "'Arf a mo' while I tell the cabby where to drive to."

He went to the back o' the cab, and afore I knew wot had 'appened the 'orse had got a flick over the head with the whip and was going along at a gallop. I kept putting the little flap up and telling the cabby to stop, but he didn't take the slightest notice. Arter I'd done it three times he kept it down so as I couldn't open it.

There was a crowd round my door when the cab drove up, and in the middle of it was my missis, the woman next door, and 'er husband, wot 'ad just come 'ome. 'Arf a dozen of 'em helped me out, and afore I could say a word the cabman drove off and left me there.

I dream of it now sometimes: standing there explaining and explaining, until, just as I feel I can't bear it any longer, two policemen come up and 'elp me indoors. If they had 'elped my missis outside it would be a easier dream to have.

HOMEWARD BOUND

Mr. Hatchard's conversation for nearly a week had been confined to fault-finding and grunts, a system of treatment designed to wean Mrs. Hatchard from her besetting sin of extravagance. On other occasions the treatment had, for short periods, proved successful, but it was quite evident that his wife's constitution was becoming inured to this physic and required a change of treatment. The evidence stared at him from the mantelpiece in the shape of a pair of huge pink vases, which had certainly not been there when he left in the morning. He looked at them and breathed heavily.

"Pretty, ain't they?" said his wife, nodding at them.

"Who gave 'em to you?" inquired Mr. Hatchard, sternly.

His wife shook her head. "You don't get vases like that given to you," she said, slowly. "Leastways, I don't."

"Do you mean to say you bought 'em?" demanded her husband.

Mrs. Hatchard nodded.

"After all I said to you about wasting my money?" persisted Mr. Hatchard, in amazed accents.

Mrs. Hatchard nodded, more brightly than before.

"There has got to be an end to this!" said her husband, desperately. "I won't have it! D'ye hear? I won't—have—it!"

"I bought 'em with my own money," said his wife, tossing her head.

"Your money?" said Mr. Hatchard. "To hear you talk anybody 'ud think you'd got three hundred a year, instead o' thirty. Your money ought to be spent in useful things, same as what mine is. Why should I spend my money keeping you, while you waste yours on pink vases and having friends in to tea?"

Mrs. Hatchard's still comely face took on a deeper tinge.

"Keeping me?" she said, sharply. "You'd better stop before you say anything you might be sorry for, Alfred."

"I should have to talk a long time before I said that," retorted the other.

"I'm not so sure," said his wife. "I'm beginning to be tired of it."

"I've reasoned with you," continued Mr. Hatchard, "I've argued with you, and I've pointed out the error of your ways to you, and it's all no good."

"Oh, be quiet, and don't talk nonsense," said his wife.

"Talking," continued Mr. Hatchard, "as I said before, is no good. Deeds, not words, is what is wanted."

He rose suddenly from his chair and, taking one of the vases from the mantelpiece, dashed it to pieces on the fender. Example is contagious, and two seconds later he was in his chair again, softly feeling a rapidly growing bump on his head, and gazing goggle-eyed at his wife.

"And I'd do it again," said that lady, breathlessly, "if there was another vase."

Mr. Hatchard opened his mouth, but speech failed him. He got up and left the room without a word, and, making his way to the scullery, turned on the tap and held his head beneath it. A sharp intake of the breath announced that a tributary stream was looking for the bump down the neck of his shirt.

He was away a long time—so long that the half-penitent Mrs. Hatchard was beginning to think of giving first aid to the wounded. Then she heard him coming slowly back along the passage. He entered the room, drying his wet hair on a hand-kerchief.

"I—I hope I didn't hurt you—much?" said his wife.

Mr. Hatchard drew himself up and regarded her with lofty indignation.

"You might have killed me," he said at last, in thrilling tones. "Then what would you have done?"

"Swept up the pieces, and said you came home injured and died in my arms," said Mrs. Hatchard, glibly. "I don't want to be unfeeling, but you'd try the temper of a saint. I'm sure I wonder I haven't done it before. Why I married a stingy man I don't know."

"Why I married at all I don't know," said her husband, in a deep voice.

"We were both fools," said Mrs. Hatchard, in a resigned voice; "that's what it was. However, it can't be helped now."

"Some men would go and leave you," said Mr. Hatchard.

"Well, go," said his wife, bridling. "I don't want you."

"Don't talk nonsense," said the other.

"It ain't nonsense," said Mrs. Hatchard. "If you want to go, go. I don't want to keep you."

"I only wish I could," said her husband, wistfully.

"There's the door," said Mrs. Hatchard, pointing. "What's to prevent you?"

"And have you going to the magistrate?" observed Mr. Hatchard.

"Not me," was the reply.

"Or coming up, full of complaints, to the ware-house?"

"Not me," said his wife again.

"It makes my mouth water to think of it," said Mr. Hatchard. "Four years ago I hadn't a care in the world."

"Me neither," said Mrs. Hatchard; "but then I never thought I should marry you. I remember the first time I saw you I had to stuff my handkerchief in my mouth."

"What for?" inquired Mr. Hatchard.

"Keep from laughing," was the reply.

"You took care not to let me see you laugh," said Mr. Hatchard, grimly. "You were polite enough in them days. I only wish I could have my time over again; that's all."

"You can go, as I said before," said his wife.

"I'd go this minute," said Mr. Hatchard, "but I know what it 'ud be: in three or four days you'd be coming and begging me to take you back again."

"You try me," said Mrs. Hatchard, with a hard laugh. "I can keep myself. You leave me the furniture—most of it is mine—and I sha'n't worry you again."

"Mind!" said Mr. Hatchard, raising his hand with great solemnity. "If I go, I never come back again."

"I'll take care of that," said his wife, equably. "You are far more likely to ask to come back than I am."

Mr. Hatchard stood for some time in deep thought, and then, spurred on by a short, contemptuous laugh from his wife, went to the small passage and, putting on his overcoat and hat, stood in the parlor doorway regarding her.

"I've a good mind to take you at your word," he said, at last.

"Good-night," said his wife, briskly. "If you send me your address, I'll send your things on to you. There's no need for you to call about them."

Hardly realizing the seriousness of the step, Mr. Hatchard closed the front door behind him with a bang, and then discovered that it was raining. Too proud to return for his umbrella, he turned up his coat-collar and, thrusting his hands in his pockets, walked slowly down the desolate little street. By the time he had walked a dozen yards he began to think that he might as well have waited until the morning; before he had walked fifty he was certain of it.

He passed the night at a coffee-house, and rose so early in the morning that the proprietor took it as a personal affront, and advised him to get his breakfast elsewhere. It was the longest day in Mr.

Hatchard's experience, and, securing modest lodgings that evening, he overslept himself and was late at the warehouse next morning for the first time in ten years.

His personal effects arrived next day, but no letter came from his wife, and one which he wrote concerning a pair of missing garments received no reply. He wrote again, referring to them in laudatory terms, and got a brief reply to the effect that they had been exchanged in part payment on a pair of valuable pink vases, the pieces of which he could have by paying the carriage.

In six weeks Mr. Hatchard changed his lodgings twice. A lack of those home comforts which he had taken as a matter of course during his married life was a source of much tribulation, and it was clear that his weekly bills were compiled by a clever writer of fiction. It was his first experience of lodgings, and the difficulty of saying unpleasant things to a woman other than his wife was not the least of his troubles. He changed his lodgings for a third time, and, much surprised at his wife's continued silence, sought out a cousin of hers named Joe Pett, and poured his troubles into that gentleman's reluctant ear.

"If she was to ask me to take her back," he concluded, "I'm not sure, mind you, that I wouldn't do so."

"It does you credit," said Mr. Pett. "Well, ta-ta; I must be off."

"And I expect she'd be very much obliged to anybody that told her so," said Mr. Hatchard, clutching at the other's sleeve.

Mr. Pett, gazing into space, said that he thought it highly probable.

"It wants to be done cleverly, though," said Mr. Hatchard, "else she might get the idea that I wanted to go back."

"I s'pose you know she's moved?" said Mr. Pett, with the air of a man anxious to change the conversation.

"Eh?" said the other.

"Number thirty-seven, John Street," said Mr. Pett. "Told my wife she's going to take in lodgers. Calling herself Mrs. Harris, after her maiden name."

He went off before Mr. Hatchard could recover, and the latter at once verified the information in part by walking round to his old house. Bits of straw and paper littered the front garden, the blinds were down, and a bill was pasted on the front parlor window. Aghast at such determination, he walked back to his lodgings in gloomy thought.

On Saturday afternoon he walked round to John Street, and from the corner of his eye, as he passed, stole a glance at No. 37. He recognized the curtains at once, and, seeing that there was nobody in the room, leaned over the palings and peered at a card that stood on the window-sash:

He walked away whistling, and after going a little way turned and passed it again. He passed in all four times, and then, with an odd grin lurking at the corners of his mouth, strode up to the front door and knocked loudly. He heard somebody moving about inside, and, more with the idea of keeping his courage up than anything else, gave another heavy knock at the door. It was thrown open hastily, and the astonished face of his wife appeared before him.

"What do you want?" she inquired, sharply.

Mr. Hatchard raised his hat. "Good-afternoon, ma'am," he said, politely.

"What do you want?" repeated his wife.

"I called," said Mr. Hatchard, clearing his throat—"I called about the bill in the window."

Mrs. Hatchard clutched at the door-post.

"Well?" she gasped.

"I'd like to see the rooms," said the other.

"But you ain't a single young man," said his wife, recovering.

"I'm as good as single," said Mr. Hatchard. "I should say, better."

"You ain't young," objected Mrs. Hatchard. "I'm three years younger than what you are," said Mr. Hatchard, dispassionately.

His wife's lips tightened and her hand closed on the door; Mr. Hatchard put his foot in.

"If you don't want lodgers, why do you put a bill up?" he inquired.

"I don't take the first that comes," said his wife.

"I'll pay a week in advance," said Mr. Hatchard, putting his hand in his pocket. "Of course, if you're afraid of having me here—afraid o' giving way to tenderness, I mean—"

"Afraid?" choked Mrs. Hatchard. "Tenderness! I—I—"

"Just a matter o' business," continued her husband; "that's my way of looking at it—that's a man's way. I s'pose women are different. They can't—"

"Come in," said Mrs. Hatchard, breathing hard Mr. Hatchard obeyed, and clapping a hand over his mouth ascended the stairs behind her. At the top she threw open the door of a tiny bedroom, and stood aside for him to enter. Mr. Hatchard sniffed critically.

"Smells rather stuffy," he said, at last.

"You needn't have it," said his wife, abruptly. "There's plenty of other fish in the sea."

"Yes; and I expect they'd stay there if they saw this room," said the other.

"Don't think I want you to have it; because I don't," said Mrs. Hatchard, making a preliminary movement to showing him downstairs.

"They might suit me," said Mr. Hatchard, musingly, as he peeped in at the sitting-room door. "I shouldn't be at home much. I'm a man that's fond of spending his evenings out."

Mrs. Hatchard, checking a retort, eyed him grimly.

"I've seen worse," he said, slowly; "but then I've seen a good many. How much are you asking?"

"Seven shillings a week," replied his wife. "With breakfast, tea, and supper, a pound a week."

Mr. Hatchard nearly whistled, but checked himself just in time.

"I'll give it a trial," he said, with an air of unbearable patronage.

Mrs. Hatchard hesitated.

"If you come here, you quite understand it's on a business footing," she said.

"O' course," said the other, with affected surprise. "What do you think I want it on?"

"You come here as a stranger, and I look after you as a stranger," continued his wife.

"Certainly," said the other. "I shall be made more comfortable that way, I'm sure. But, of course, if you're afraid, as I said before, of giving way to tender—"

"Tender fiddlesticks!" interrupted his wife, flushing and eying him angrily.

"I'll come in and bring my things at nine o'clock to-night," said Mr. Hatchard. "I'd like the windows open and the rooms aired a bit. And what about the sheets?"

"What about them?" inquired his wife.

"Don't put me in damp sheets, that's all," said Mr. Hatchard. "One place I was at—"

He broke off suddenly.

"Well!" said his wife, quickly.

"Was very particular about them," said Mr. Hatchard, recovering. "Well, good-afternoon to you, ma'am."

"I want three weeks in advance," said his wife. "Three—" exclaimed the other. "Three weeks in advance? Why—"

"Those are my terms," said Mrs. Hatchard. "Take 'em or leave 'em. P'r'aps it would be better if you left 'em."

Mr. Hatchard looked thoughtful, and then with obvious reluctance took his purse from one pocket and some silver from another, and made up the required sum.

"And what if I'm not comfortable here?" he inquired, as his wife hastily pocketed the money. "It'll be your own fault," was the reply.

Mr. Hatchard looked dubious, and, in a thoughtful fashion, walked downstairs and let himself out. He began to think that the joke was of a more complicated nature than he had expected, and it was not without forebodings that he came back at nine o'clock that night accompanied by a boy with his baggage.

His gloom disappeared the moment the door opened. The air inside was warm and comfortable, and pervaded by an appetizing smell of cooked meats. Upstairs a small bright fire and a neatly laid supper-table awaited his arrival.

He sank into an easy-chair and rubbed his hands. Then his gaze fell on a small bell on the table, and opening the door he rang for supper.

"Yes, sir," said Mrs. Hatchard, entering the room. "Supper, please," said the new lodger, with dignity.

Mrs. Hatchard looked bewildered. "Well, there it is," she said, indicating the table. "You don't want me to feed you, do you?"

The lodger eyed the small, dry piece of cheese, the bread and butter, and his face fell. "I—I thought I smelled something cooking," he said at last.

"Oh, that was my supper," said Mrs. Hatchard, with a smile.

"I—I'm very hungry," said Mr. Hatchard, trying to keep his temper.

"It's the cold weather, I expect," said Mrs. Hatchard, thoughtfully; "it does affect some people that way, I know. Please ring if you want anything."

She left the room, humming blithely, and Mr. Hatchard, after sitting for some time in silent consternation, got up and ate his frugal meal. The fact that the water-jug held three pints and was filled to the brim gave him no satisfaction.

He was still hungry when he arose next morning, and, with curiosity tempered by uneasiness, waited for his breakfast. Mrs. Hatchard came in at last, and after polite inquiries as to how he had slept proceeded to lay breakfast. A fresh loaf and a large teapot appeared, and the smell of frizzling bacon ascended from below. Then Mrs. Hatchard came in again, and, smiling benevolently, placed an egg before him and withdrew. Two minutes later he rang the bell.

"You can clear away," he said, as Mrs. Hatchard entered the room.

"What, no breakfast?" she said, holding up her hands. "Well, I've heard of you single young men, but I never thought—"

"The tea's cold and as black as ink," growled the indignant lodger, "and the egg isn't eatable."

"I'm afraid you're a bit of a fault-finder," said Mrs. Hatchard, shaking her head at him. "I'm sure I try my best to please. I don't mind what I do, but if you're not satisfied you'd better go."

"Look here, Emily—" began her husband.

"Don't you 'Emily' me!" said Mrs. Hatchard, quickly. "The idea! A lodger, too! You know the arrangement. You'd better go, I think, if you can't behave yourself."

"I won't go till my three weeks are up," said Mr. Hatchard, doggedly, "so you may as well behave yourself."

"I can't pamper you for a pound a week," said Mrs. Hatchard, walking to the door. "If you want pampering, you had better go."

A week passed, and the additional expense caused by getting most of his meals out began to affect Mr. Hatchard's health. His wife, on the contrary, was in excellent spirits, and, coming in one day, explained the absence of the easy-chair by stating that it was wanted for a new lodger.

"He's taken my other two rooms," she said, smiling—"the little back parlor and the front bedroom—I'm full up now."

"Wouldn't he like my table, too?" inquired Mr. Hatchard, with bitter sarcasm.

His wife said that she would inquire, and brought back word next day that Mr. Sadler, the new lodger, would like it. It disappeared during Mr. Hatchard's enforced absence at business, and a small bamboo table, weak in the joints, did duty in its stead.

The new lodger, a man of middle age with a ready tongue, was a success from the first, and it was only too evident that Mrs. Hatchard was trying her best to please him. Mr. Hatchard, supping on bread and cheese, more than once left that wholesome meal to lean over the balusters and smell the hot meats going into Mr. Sadler.

"You're spoiling him," he said to Mrs. Hatchard, after the new lodger had been there a week. "Mark my words—he'll get above himself."

"That's my look-out," said his wife briefly. "Don't come to me if you get into trouble, that's all," said the other.

Mrs. Hatchard laughed derisively. "You don't like him, that's what it is," she remarked. "He asked me yesterday whether he had offended you in any way."

"Oh! He did, did he?" snarled Mr. Hatchard. "Let him keep himself to himself, and mind his own business."

"He said he thinks you have got a bad temper," continued his wife. "He thinks, perhaps, it's indigestion, caused by eating cheese for supper always."

Mr. Hatchard affected not to hear, and, lighting his pipe, listened fer some time to the hum of conversation between his wife and Mr. Sadler below. With an expression of resignation on his face that was almost saintly he knocked out his pipe at last and went to bed.

Half an hour passed, and he was still awake. His wife's voice had ceased, but the gruff tones of Mr. Sadler were still audible. Then he sat up in bed and listened, as a faint cry of alarm and the sound of somebody rushing upstairs fell on his ears. The next moment the door of his room burst open, and a wild figure, stumbling in the darkness, rushed over to the bed and clasped him in its arms.

"Help!" gasped his wile's voice. "Oh, Alfred! Alfred!"

"Ma'am!" said Mr. Hatchard in a prim voice, as he struggled in vain to free himself.

"I'm so—so—fr-frightened!" sobbed Mrs. Hatchard.

"That's no reason for coming into a lodger's room and throwing your arms round his neck," said her husband, severely.

"Don't be stu-stu-stupid," gasped Mrs. Hatchard. "He—he's sitting downstairs in my room with a paper cap on his head and a fire-shovel in his hand, and he—he says he's the—the Emperor of China."

"He? Who?" inquired her husband.

"Mr. Sad-Sadler," replied Mrs. Hatchard, almost strangling him. "He made me kneel in front o' him and keep touching the floor with my head."

The chair-bedstead shook in sympathy with Mr. Hatchard's husbandly emotion.

"Well, it's nothing to do with me," he said at last.

"He's mad," said his wife, in a tense whisper; "stark staring mad. He says I'm his favorite wife, and he made me stroke his forehead."

The bed shook again.

"I don't see that I have any right to interfere," said Mr. Hatchard, after he had quieted the bedstead. "He's your lodger."

"You're my husband," said Mrs. Hatchard. "Ho!" said Mr. Hatchard. "You've remembered that, have you?"

"Yes, Alfred," said his wife.

"And are you sorry for all your bad behavior?" demanded Mr. Hatchard.

Mrs. Hatchard hesitated. Then a clatter of fire-irons downstairs moved her to speech.

"Ye-yes," she sobbed.

"And you want me to take you back?" queried the generous Mr. Hatchard.

"Ye-ye-yes," said his wife.

Mr. Hatchard got out of bed and striking a match lit the candle, and, taking his overcoat from a peg behind the door, put it on and marched downstairs. Mrs. Hatchard, still trembling, followed behind.

"What's all this?" he demanded, throwing the door open with a flourish.

Mr. Sadler, still holding the fire-shovel sceptre-fashion and still with the paper cap on his head, opened his mouth to reply. Then, as he saw the unkempt figure of Mr. Hatchard with the scared face of Mrs. Hatchard peeping over his shoulder, his face grew red, his eyes watered, and his cheeks swelled.

"K-K-K-Kch! K-Kch!" he said, explosively. "Talk English, not Chinese," said Mr. Hatchard, sternly.

Mr. Sadler threw down the fire-shovel, and to Mr. Hatchard's great annoyance, clapped his open hand over his mouth and rocked with merriment.

"Sh—sh—she—she—" he spluttered.

"That'll do," said Mr. Hatchard, hastily, with a warning frown.

"Kow-towed to me," gurgled Mr. Sadler. "You ought to have seen it, Alf. I shall never get over it—never. It's—no—no good win-winking at me; I can't help myself."

He put his handkerchief to his eyes and leaned back exhausted. When he removed it, he found himself alone and everything still but for a murmur of voices overhead. Anon steps sounded on the stairs, and Mr. Hatchard, grave of face, entered the room.

"Outside!" he said, briefly.

"What!" said the astounded Mr. Sadler. "Why, it's eleven o'clock."

"I can't help it if it's twelve o'clock," was the reply. "You shouldn't play the fool and spoil things by laughing. Now, are you going, or have I got to put you out?"

He crossed the room and, putting his hand on the shoulder of the protesting Mr. Sadler, pushed him into the passage, and taking his coat from the peg held it up for him. Mr. Sadler, abandoning himself to his fate, got into it slowly and indulged in a few remarks on the subject of ingratitude.

"I can't help it," said his friend, in a low voice. "I've had to swear I've never seen you before."

"Does she believe you?" said the staring Mr. Sadler, shivering at the open door.

"No," said Mr. Hatchard, slowly, "but she pre-tends to."

HUSBANDRY

Dealing with a man, said the night-watchman, thoughtfully, is as easy as a teetotaller walking along a nice wide pavement; dealing with a woman is like the same teetotaller, arter four or five whiskies, trying to get up a step that ain't there. If a man can't get 'is own way he eases 'is mind with a little nasty language, and then forgets all about it; if a woman can't get 'er own way she flies into a temper and reminds you of something you oughtn't to ha' done ten years ago. Wot a woman would do whose 'usband had never done anything wrong I can't think.

I remember a young feller telling me about a row he 'ad with 'is wife once. He 'adn't been married long and he talked as if the way she carried on was unusual. Fust of all, he said, she spoke to 'im in a cooing sort o' voice and pulled his moustache, then when he wouldn't give way she worked herself up into a temper and said things about 'is sister. Arter which she went out o' the room and banged the door so hard it blew down a vase off the fireplace. Four times she came back to tell 'im other things she 'ad thought of, and then she got so upset she 'ad to go up to bed and lay down instead of getting his tea. When that didn't do no good she refused her food, and when 'e took her up toast and tea she wouldn't look at it. Said she wanted to die. He got quite uneasy till 'e came 'ome the next night and found the best part of a loaf o' bread, a quarter o' butter, and a couple o' chops he 'ad got in for 'is supper had gorn; and then when he said 'e was glad she 'ad got 'er appetite back she turned round and said that he grudged 'er the food she ate.

And no woman ever owned up as 'ow she was wrong; and the more you try and prove it to 'em the louder they talk about something else. I know wot I'm talking about because a woman made a mistake about me once, and though she was proved to be in the wrong, and it was years ago, my missus shakes her 'ead about it to this day.

It was about eight years arter I 'ad left off going to sea and took up night-watching. A beautiful summer evening it was, and I was sitting by the gate smoking a pipe till it should be time to light up, when I noticed a woman who 'ad just passed turn back and stand staring at me. I've 'ad that sort o' thing before, and I went on smoking and looking straight in front of me. Fat middle-aged woman she was, wot 'ad lost her good looks and found others. She stood there staring and staring, and by and by she tries a little cough.

I got up very slow then, and, arter looking all round at the evening, without seeing 'er, I was just going to step inside and shut the wicket, when she came closer.

"Bill!" she ses, in a choking sort o' voice.

"Bill!"

I gave her a look that made her catch 'er breath, and I was just stepping through the wicket, when she laid hold of my coat and tried to hold me back.

"Do you know wot you're a-doing of?" I ses, turning on her.

"Oh, Bill dear," she ses, "don't talk to me like that. Do you want to break my 'art? Arter all these years!"

She pulled out a dirt-coloured pocket-'ankercher and stood there dabbing her eyes with it. One eye at a time she dabbed, while she looked at me reproachful with the other. And arter eight dabs, four to each eye, she began to sob as if her 'art would break.

"Go away," I ses, very slow. "You can't stand making that noise outside my wharf. Go away and give somebody else a treat."

Afore she could say anything the potman from the Tiger, a nasty ginger-'aired little chap that nobody liked, come by and stopped to pat her on the back.

"There, there, don't take on, mother," he ses. "Wot's he been a-doing to you?"

"You get off 'ome," I ses, losing my temper.

"Wot d'ye mean trying to drag me into it? I've never seen the woman afore in my life."

"Oh, Bill!" ses the woman, sobbing louder than ever. "Oh! Oh! Oh!"

"'Ow does she know your name, then?" ses the little beast of a potman.

I didn't answer him. I might have told 'im that there's about five million Bills in England, but I didn't. I stood there with my arms folded acrost my chest, and looked at him, superior.

"Where 'ave you been all this long, long time?" she ses, between her sobs. "Why did you leave your happy 'ome and your children wot loved you?"

The potman let off a whistle that you could have 'eard acrost the river, and as for me, I thought I should ha' dropped. To have a woman standing sobbing and taking my character away like that was a'most more than I could bear.

"Did he run away from you?" ses the potman.

"Ye-ye-yes," she ses. "He went off on a vy'ge to China over nine years ago, and that's the last I saw of 'im till to-night. A lady friend o' mine thought she reckernized 'im yesterday, and told me."

"I shouldn't cry over 'im," ses the potman, shaking his 'ead: "he ain't worth it. If I was you I should just give 'im a bang or two over the 'ead with my umberella, and then give 'im in charge."

I stepped inside the wicket—backwards—and then I slammed it in their faces, and putting the key in my pocket, walked up the wharf. I knew it was no good standing out there argufying. I felt sorry for the pore thing in a way. If she really thought I was her 'usband, and she 'ad lost me—I put one or two things straight and then, for the sake of distracting my mind, I 'ad a word or two with the skipper of the John Henry, who was leaning against the side of his ship, smoking.

"Wot's that tapping noise?" he ses, all of a sudden. "'Ark!"

I knew wot it was. It was the handle of that umberella 'ammering on the gate. I went cold all over, and then when I thought that the pot-man was most likely encouraging 'er to do it I began to boil.

"Somebody at the gate," ses the skipper.

"Aye, aye," I ses. "I know all about it."

I went on talking until at last the skipper asked me whether he was wandering in 'is mind, or whether I was. The mate came up from the cabin just then, and o' course he 'ad to tell me there was somebody knocking at the gate.

"Ain't you going to open it?" ses the skipper, staring at me.

"Let 'em ring," I ses, off-hand.

The words was 'ardly out of my mouth afore they did ring, and if they 'ad been selling muffins they couldn't ha' kept it up harder. And all the time the umberella was doing rat-a-tat tats on the gate, while a voice— much too loud for the potman's—started calling out: "Watch-man ahoy!"

"They're calling you, Bill," ses the skipper. "I ain't deaf," I ses, very cold.

"Well, I wish I was," ses the skipper. "It's fair making my ear ache. Why the blazes don't you do your dooty, and open the gate?"

"You mind your bisness and I'll mind mine," I ses. "I know wot I'm doing. It's just some silly fools 'aving a game with me, and I'm not going to encourage 'em."

"Game with you?" ses the skipper. "Ain't they got anything better than that to play with? Look 'ere, if you don't open that gate, I will."

"It's nothing to do with you," I ses. "You look arter your ship and I'll look arter my wharf. See? If you don't like the noise, go down in the cabin and stick your 'ead in a biscuit-bag."

To my surprise he took the mate by the arm and went, and I was just thinking wot a good thing it was to be a bit firm with people sometimes, when they came back dressed up in their coats and bowler-hats and climbed on to the wharf.

"Watchman!" ses the skipper, in a hoity-toity sort o' voice, "me and the mate is going as far as Aldgate for a breath o' fresh air. Open the gate."

I gave him a look that might ha' melted a 'art of stone, and all it done to 'im was to make 'im laugh.

"Hurry up," he ses. "It a'most seems to me that there's somebody ringing the bell, and you can let them in same time as you let us out. Is it the bell, or is it my fancy, Joe?" he ses, turning to the mate.

They marched on in front of me with their noses cocked in the air, and all the time the noise at the gate got worse and worse. So far as I could make out, there was quite a crowd outside, and I stood there with the key in the lock, trembling all over. Then I unlocked it very careful, and put my hand on the skipper's arm.

"Nip out quick," I ses, in a whisper.

"I'm in no hurry," ses the skipper. "Here! Halloa, wot's up?"

It was like opening the door at a theatre, and the fust one through was that woman, shoved behind by the potman. Arter 'im came a car-man, two big 'ulking brewers' draymen, a little scrap of a woman with 'er bonnet cocked over one eye, and a couple of dirty little boys.

"Wot is it?" ses the skipper, shutting the wicket behind 'em. "A beanfeast?"

"This lady wants her 'usband," ses the pot-man, pointing at me. "He run away from her nine years ago, and now he says he 'as never seen 'er before. He ought to be 'ung."

"Bill," ses the skipper, shaking his silly 'ead at me. "I can 'ardly believe it."

"It's all a pack o' silly lies," I ses, firing up. "She's made a mistake."

"She made a mistake when she married you," ses the thin little woman. "If I was in 'er shoes I'd take 'old of you and tear you limb from limb."

"I don't want to hurt 'im, ma'am," ses the other woman. "I on'y want him to come 'ome to me and my five. Why, he's never seen the youngest, little Annie. She's as like 'im as two peas."

"Pore little devil," ses the carman.

"Look here!" I ses, "you clear off. All of you. 'Ow dare you come on to my wharf? If you aren't gone in two minutes I'll give you all in charge."

"Who to?" ses one of the draymen, sticking his face into mine. "You go 'ome to your wife and kids. Go on now, afore I put up my 'ands to you."

"That's the way to talk to 'im," ses the pot-man, nodding at 'em.

They all began to talk to me then and tell me wot I was to do, and wot they would do if I didn't. I couldn't get a word in edgeways. When I reminded the mate that when he was up in London 'e always passed himself off as a single man, 'e wouldn't listen; and when I asked the skipper whether 'is pore missus was blind, he on'y went on shouting at the top of 'is voice. It on'y showed me 'ow anxious most people are that everybody else should be good.

I thought they was never going to stop, and, if it 'adn't been for a fit of coughing, I don't believe that the scraggy little woman could ha' stopped. Arter one o' the draymen 'ad saved her life and spoilt 'er temper by patting 'er on the back with a hand the size of a leg o' mutton, the carman turned to me and told me to tell the truth, if it choked me.

"I have told you the truth," I ses. "She ses I'm her 'usband and I say I ain't. Ow's she going to prove it? Why should you believe her, and not me?"

"She's got a truthful face," ses the carman.

"Look here!" ses the skipper, speaking very slow, "I've got an idea, wot'll settle it p'raps. You get outside," he ses, turning sharp on the two little boys.

One o' the draymen 'elped 'em to go out, and 'arf a minute arterwards a stone came over the gate and cut the potman's lip open. Boys will be boys.

"Now!" ses the skipper, turning to the woman, and smiling with conceitedness. "Had your 'usband got any marks on 'im? Birth-mark, or moles, or anything of that sort?"

"I'm sure he is my 'usband," ses the woman, dabbing her eyes.

"Yes, yes," ses the skipper, "but answer my question. If you can tell us any marks your 'usband had, we can take Bill down into my cabin and—"

"You'll do WOT?" I ses, in a loud voice.

"You speak when you're spoke to," ses the carman. "It's got nothing to do with you."

"No, he ain't got no birthmarks," ses the woman, speaking very slow—and I could see she was afraid of making a mistake and losing me—"but he's got tattoo marks. He's got a mermaid tattooed on 'im."

"Where?" ses the skipper, a'most jumping.

I 'eld my breath. Five sailormen out of ten have been tattooed with mermaids, and I was one of 'em. When she spoke agin I thought I should ha' dropped.

"On 'is right arm," she ses, "unless he's 'ad it rubbed off."

"You can't rub out tattoo marks," ses the skipper.

They all stood looking at me as if they was waiting for something. I folded my arms—tight—and stared back at 'em.

"If you ain't this lady's 'usband," ses the skipper, turning to me, "you can take off your coat and prove it."

"And if you don't we'll take it off for you," ses the carman, coming a bit closer.

Arter that things 'appened so quick, I hardly knew whether I was standing on my 'cad or my heels. Both, I think. They was all on top o' me at once, and the next thing I can remember is sitting on the ground in my shirt-sleeves listening to the potman, who was making a fearful fuss because somebody 'ad bit his ear 'arf off. My coat was ripped up the back, and one of the draymen was holding up my arm and showing them all the mermaid, while the other struck matches so as they could see better."

"That's your 'usband right enough," he ses to the woman. "Take 'im."

"P'raps she'll carry 'im 'ome," I ses, very fierce and sarcastic.

"And we don't want none of your lip," ses the carman, who was in a bad temper because he 'ad got a fearful kick on the shin from somewhere.

I got up very slow and began to put my coat on again, and twice I 'ad to tell that silly woman that when I wanted her 'elp I'd let 'er know. Then I 'eard slow, heavy footsteps in the road outside, and, afore any of 'em could stop me, I was calling for the police.

I don't like policemen as a rule; they're too inquisitive, but when the wicket was pushed open and I saw a face with a helmet on it peeping in, I felt quite a liking for 'em.

"Wot's up?" ses the policeman, staring 'ard at my little party.

They all started telling 'im at once, and I should think if the potman showed him 'is ear once he showed it to 'im twenty times. He lost his temper and pushed it away at last, and the potman gave a 'owl that set my teeth on edge. I waited till they was all finished, and the policeman trying to get 'is hearing back, and then I spoke up in a quiet way and told 'im to clear them all off of my wharf.

"They're trespassing," I ses, "all except the skipper and mate here. They belong to a little wash-tub that's laying alongside, and they're both as 'armless as they look."

It's wonderful wot a uniform will do. The policeman just jerked his 'ead and said "out-side," and the men went out like a flock of sheep. The on'y man that said a word was the carman, who was in such a hurry that 'e knocked his bad shin against my foot as 'e went by. The thin little woman was passed out by the policeman in the middle of a speech she was making, and he was just going for the other, when the skipper stopped 'im.

"This lady is coming on my ship," he ses, puffing out 'is chest.

I looked at 'im, and then I turned to the policeman. "So long as she goes off my wharf, I don't mind where she goes," I ses. "The skipper's goings-on 'ave got nothing to do with me."

"Then she can foller him 'ome in the morning," ses the skipper. "Good night, watch-man."

Him and the mate 'elped the silly old thing to the ship, and, arter I 'ad been round to the Bear's Head and fetched a pint for the police-man, I locked up and sat down to think things out; and the more I thought the worse they seemed. I've 'eard people say that if you have a clear conscience nothing can hurt you. They didn't know my missus.

I got up at last and walked on to the jetty, and the woman, wot was sitting on the deck of the John Henry, kept calling out: "Bill!" like a sick baa-lamb crying for its ma. I went back, and 'ad four pints at the Bear's Head, but it didn't seem to do me any good, and at last I went and sat down in the office to wait for morning.

It came at last, a lovely morning with a beautiful sunrise; and that woman sitting up wide awake, waiting to foller me 'ome. When I opened the gate at six o'clock she was there with the mate and the skipper, waiting, and when I left at five minutes past she was trotting along beside me.

Twice I stopped and spoke to 'er, but it was no good. Other people stopped too, and I 'ad to move on agin; and every step was bringing me nearer to my house and the missus.

I turned into our street, arter passing it three times, and the first thing I saw was my missus standing on the doorstep 'aving a few words with the lady next door. Then she 'appened to look up and see us, just as that silly woman was trying to walk arm-in-arm.

Twice I knocked her 'and away, and then, right afore my wife and the party next door, she put her arm round my waist. By the time I got to the 'ouse my legs was trembling so I could hardly stand, and when I got into the passage I 'ad to lean up against the wall for a bit.

"Keep 'er out," I ses.

"Wot do you want?" ses my missus, trembling with passion. "Wot do you think you're doing?"

"I want my 'usband, Bill," ses the woman.

My missus put her 'and to her throat and came in without a word, and the woman follered 'er. If I hadn't kept my presence o' mind and shut the door two or three more would 'ave come in too.

I went into the kitchen about ten minutes arterwards to see 'ow they was getting on. Besides which they was both calling for me.

"Now then!" ses my missus, who was leaning up against the dresser with 'er arms folded, "wot 'ave you got to say for yourself walking in as bold as brass with this hussy?"

"Bill!" ses the woman, "did you hear wot she called me?"

She spoke to me like that afore my wife, and in two minutes they was at it, hammer and tongs.

Fust of all they spoke about each other, and then my missus started speaking about me. She's got a better memory than most people, because she can remember things that never 'appened, and every time I coughed she turned on me like a tiger.

"And as for you," she ses, turning to the woman, "if you did marry 'im you should ha' made sure that he 'adn't got a wife already."

"He married me fust," ses the woman.

"When?" ses my wife. "Wot was the date?"

"Wot was the date you married 'im?" ses the other one.

They stood looking at each other like a couple o' game-cocks, and I could see as plain as a pike-staff 'ow frightened both of 'em was o' losing me.

"Look here!" I ses at last, to my missus, "talk sense. 'Ow could I be married to 'er? When I was at sea I was at sea, and when I was ashore I was with you."

"Did you use to go down to the ship to see 'im off?" ses the woman.

"No," ses my wife. "I'd something better to do."

"Neither did I," ses the woman. "P'raps that's where we both made a mistake."

"You get out of my 'ouse!" ses my missus, very sudden. "Go on, afore I put you out."

"Not without my Bill," ses the woman. "If you lay a finger on me I'll scream the house down."

"You brought her 'ere," ses my wife, turning to me, "now you can take 'er away?"

"I didn't bring 'er," I ses. "She follered me."

"Well, she can foller you agin," she ses. "Go on!" she ses, trembling all over. "Git out afore I start on you."

I was in such a temper that I daren't trust myself to stop. I just gave 'er one look, and then I drew myself up and went out. 'Alf the fools in our street was standing in front of the 'ouse, 'umming like bees, but I took no notice. I held my 'ead up and walked through them with that woman trailing arter me.

I was in such a state of mind that I went on like a man in a dream. If it had ha' been a dream I should ha' pushed 'er under an omnibus, but you can't do things like that in real life.

"Penny for your thoughts, Bill," she ses. I didn't answer her.

"Why don't you speak to me?" she ses.

"You don't know wot you're asking for," I ses.

I was hungry and sleepy, and 'ow I was going to get through the day I couldn't think. I went into a pub and 'ad a couple o' pints o' stout and a crust o' bread and cheese for brekfuss. I don't know wot she 'ad, but when the barman tried to take for it out o' my money, I surprised 'im.

We walked about till I was ready to drop. Then we got to Victoria Park, and I 'ad no sooner got on to the grass than I laid down and went straight off to sleep. It was two o'clock when I woke, and, arter a couple o' pork-pies and a pint or two, I sat on a seat in the Park smoking, while she kep' dabbing 'er eyes agin and asking me to come 'ome.

At five o'clock I got up to go back to the wharf, and, taking no notice of 'er, I walked into the street and jumped on a 'bus that was passing. She jumped too, and, arter the conductor had 'elped 'er up off of 'er knees and taken her arms away from his waist, I'm blest if he didn't turn on me and ask me why I 'adn't left her at 'ome.

We got to the wharf just afore six. The John Henry 'ad gorn, but the skipper 'ad done all the 'arm he could afore he sailed, and, if I 'adn't kept my temper, I should ha' murdered arf a dozen of 'em.

The woman wanted to come on to the wharf, but I 'ad a word or two with one o' the fore-men, who owed me arf-a-dollar, and he made that all right.

"We all 'ave our faults, Bill," he ses as 'e went out, "and I suppose she was better looking once upon a time?"

I didn't answer 'im. I shut the wicket arter 'im, quick, and turned the key, and then I went on with my work. For a long time everything was as quiet as the grave, and then there came just one little pull at the bell. Five minutes arterwards there was another.

I thought it was that woman, but I 'ad to make sure. When it came the third time I crept up to the gate.

"Halloa!" I ses. "Who is it?"

"Me, darling," ses a voice I reckernized as the potman's. "Your missus wants to come in and sit down."

I could 'ear several people talking, and it seemed to me there was quite a crowd out there, and by and by that bell was going like mad. Then people started kicking the gate, and shouting, but I took no notice until, presently, it left off all of a sudden, and I 'eard a loud voice asking what it was all about. I suppose there was about fifty of 'em all telling it at once, and then there was the sound of a fist on the gate.

"Who is it?" I ses.

"Police," ses the voice.

I opened the wicket then and looked out. A couple o' policemen was standing by the gate and arf the riff-raff of Wapping behind 'em.

"Wot's all this about?" ses one o' the policemen.

I shook my 'ead. "Ask me another," I ses. "Your missus is causing a disturbance," he ses.

"She's not my missus," I ses; "she's a complete stranger to me."

"And causing a crowd to collect and refusing to go away," ses the other policeman.

"That's your business," I ses. "It's nothing to do with me."

They talked to each other for a moment, and then they spoke to the woman. I didn't 'ear wot she said, but I saw her shake her 'ead, and a'most direckly arterwards she was marching away between the two policemen with the crowd follering and advising 'er where to kick 'em.

I was a bit worried at fust—not about her—and then I began to think that p'raps it was the best thing that could have 'appened.

I went 'ome in the morning with a load lifted off my mind; but I 'adn't been in the 'ouse two seconds afore my missus started to put it on agin. Fust of all she asked me 'ow I dared to come into the 'ouse, and then she wanted to know wot I meant by leaving her at 'ome and going out for the day with another woman.

"You told me to," I ses.

"Oh, yes," she ses, trembling with temper. "You always do wot I tell you, don't you? Al-ways 'ave, especially when it's anything you like."

She fetched a bucket o' water and scrubbed the kitchen while I was having my brekfuss, but I kept my eye on 'er, and, the moment she 'ad finished, I did the perlite and emptied the bucket for 'er, to prevent mistakes.

I read about the case in the Sunday paper, and I'm thankful to say my name wasn't in it. All the magistrate done was to make 'er promise that she wouldn't do it again, and then he let 'er go. I should ha' felt more comfortable if he 'ad given 'er five years, but, as it turned out, it didn't matter. Her 'usband happened to read it, and, whether 'e was tired of living alone, or whether he was excited by 'earing that she 'ad got a little general shop, 'e went back to her.

The fust I knew about it was they came round to the wharf to see me. He 'ad been a fine-looking chap in 'is day, and even then 'e was enough like me for me to see 'ow she 'ad made the mistake; and all the time she was telling me 'ow it 'appened, he was looking me up and down and sniffing.

"'Ave you got a cold?" I ses, at last.

"Wot's that got to do with you?" he ses. "Wot do you mean by walking out with my wife? That's what I've come to talk about."

For a moment I thought that his bad luck 'ad turned 'is brain. "You've got it wrong," I ses, as soon as I could speak. "She walked out with me."

"Cos she thought you was her 'usband," he ses, "but you didn't think you was me, did you?"

"'Course I didn't," I ses.

"Then 'ow dare you walk out with 'er?" he ses.

"Look 'ere!" I ses. "You get off 'ome as quick as you like. I've 'ad about enough of your family. Go on, hook it."

Afore I could put my 'ands up he 'it me hard in the mouth, and the next moment we was at it as 'ard as we could go. Nearly every time I hit 'im he wasn't there, and every time 'e hit me I wished I hadn't ha' been. When I said I had 'ad enough, 'e contradicted me and kept on, but he got tired of it at last, and, arter telling me wot he would do if I ever walked 'is wife out agin, they went off like a couple o' love-birds.

By the time I got 'ome next morning my eyes was so swelled up I could 'ardly see, and my nose wouldn't let me touch it. I was so done up I could 'ardly speak, but I managed to tell my missus about it arter I had 'ad a cup o' tea. Judging by her face anybody might ha' thought I was telling 'er something funny, and, when I 'ad finished, she looks up at the ceiling and ses:

"I 'ope it'll be a lesson to you," she ses.

IN BORROWED PLUMES

The master of the Sarah Jane had been missing for two days, and all on board, with the exception of the boy, whom nobody troubled about, were full of joy at the circumstance. Twice before had the skipper, whose habits might, perhaps, be best described as irregular, missed his ship, and word had gone forth that the third time would be the last. His berth was a good one, and the mate wanted it in place of his own, which was wanted by Ted Jones, A. B.

"Two hours more," said the mate anxiously to the men, as they stood leaning against the side, "and I take the ship out."

"Under two hours'll do it," said Ted, peering over the side and watching the water as it slowly rose over the mud. "What's got the old man, I wonder?"

"I don't know, and I don't care," said the mate. "You chaps stand by me and it'll be good for all of us. Mr. Pearson said distinct the last time that if the skipper ever missed his ship again it would be his last trip in her, and he told me afore the old man that I wasn't to wait two minutes at any time, but to bring her out right away."

"He's an old fool," said Bill Loch, the other hand; "and nobody'll miss him but the boy, and he's been looking reg'lar worried all the morning. He looked so worried at dinner time that I give 'im a kick to cheer him up a bit. Look at him now."

The mate gave a supercilious glance in the direction of the boy, and then turned away. The boy, who had no idea of courting observation, stowed himself away behind the windlass; and, taking a letter from his pocket, perused it for the fourth time.

"Dear Tommy," it began. "I take my pen in and to inform you that I'm stayin here and cant get away for the reason that I lorst my cloes at cribage larst night, also my money, and everything beside.

Dont speek to a living sole about it as the mate wants my birth, but pack up sum cloes and bring them to me without saying nuthing to noboddy. The mates cloths will do becos I havent got enny other soot, dont tell 'im. You needen't trouble about soks as I've got them left. My bed is so bad I must now conclude. Your affecshunate uncle and captin Joe Bross. P.S. Dont let the mate see you come, or else he wont let you go."

"Two hours more," sighed Tommy, as he put the letter back in his pocket. "How can I get any clothes when they're all locked up? And aunt said I was to look after 'im and see he didn't get into no mischief."

He sat thinking deeply, and then, as the crew of the Sarah Jane stepped ashore to take advantage of a glass offered by the mate, he crept down to the cabin again for another desperate look round. The only articles of clothing visible belonged to Mrs. Bross, who up to this trip had been sailing in the schooner to look after its master. At these he gazed hard.

"I'll take 'em and try an' swop 'em for some men's clothes," said he suddenly, snatching the garments from the pegs. "She wouldn't mind"; and hastily rolling them into a parcel, together with a pair of carpet slippers of the captain's, he thrust the lot into an old biscuit bag.

Then he shouldered his burden, and, going cautiously on deck, gained the shore, and set off at a trot to the address furnished in the letter.

It was a long way, and the bag was heavy. His first attempt at barter was alarming, for the pawnbroker, who had just been cautioned by the police, was in such a severe and uncomfortable state of morals, that the boy quickly snatched up his bundle again and left. Sorely troubled he walked hastily along, until, in a small bye street, his glance fell upon a baker of mild and benevolent aspect, standing behind the counter of his shop.

"If you please, sir," said Tommy, entering, and depositing his bag on the counter, "have you got any cast-off clothes you don't want?"

The baker turned to a shelf, and selecting a stale loaf cut it in halves, one of which he placed before the boy.

"I don't want bread," said Tommy desperately; "but mother has just died, and father wants mourning for the funeral. He's only got a new suit with him, and if he can change these things of mother's for an old suit, he'd sell his best ones to bury her with."

He shook the articles out on the counter, and the baker's wife, who had just come into the shop, inspected them rather favourably.

"Poor boy, so you've lost your mother," she said, turning the clothes over. "It's a good skirt, Bill."

"Yes, ma'am," said Tommy dolefully.

"What did she die of?" inquired the baker.

"Scarlet fever," said Tommy, tearfully, mentioning the only disease he knew.

"Scar—Take them things away," yelled the baker, pushing the clothes on to the floor, and following his wife to the other end of the shop. "Take 'em away directly, you young villain."

His voice was so loud, his manner so imperative, that the startled boy, without stopping to argue, stuffed the clothes pell-mell into the bag again and departed. A farewell glance at the clock made him look almost as horrified as the baker.

"There's no time to be lost," he muttered, as he began to run; "either the old man'll have to come in these or else stay where he is."

He reached the house breathless, and paused before an unshaven man in time-worn greasy clothes, who was smoking a short clay pipe with much enjoyment in front of the door.

"Is Cap'n Bross here?" he panted.

"He's upstairs," said the man, with a leer, "sitting in sackcloth and ashes, more ashes than sackcloth. Have you got some clothes for him?"

"Look here," said Tommy. He was down on his knees with the mouth of the bag open again, quite in the style of the practised hawker. "Give me an old suit of clothes for them. Hurry up. There's a lovely frock."

"Blimey," said the man, staring, "I've only got these clothes. Wot d'yer take me for? A dook?"

"Well, get me some somewhere," said Tommy. "If you don't the cap'n 'll have to come in these, and I'm sure he won't like it."

"I wonder what he'd look like," said the man, with a grin. "Damme if I don't come up and see."

"Get me some clothes," pleaded Tommy.

"I wouldn't get you clothes, no, not for fifty pun," said the man severely. "Wot d'yer mean wanting to spoil people's pleasure in that way? Come on, come and tell the cap'n what you've got for 'im, I want to 'ear what he ses. He's been swearing 'ard since ten o'clock this morning, but he ought to say something special over this."

He led the way up the bare wooden stairs, followed by the harassed boy, and entered a small dirty room at the top, in the centre of which the master of the Sarah Jane sat to deny visitors, in a pair of socks and last week's paper.

"Here's a young gent come to bring you some clothes, cap'n," said the man, taking the sack from the boy.

"Why didn't you come before?" growled the captain, who was reading the advertisements.

The man put his hand in the sack, and pulled out the clothes. "What do you think of 'em?" he asked expectantly.

The captain strove vainly to tell him, but his tongue mercifully forsook its office, and dried between his lips. His brain rang with sentences of scorching iniquity, but they got no further.

"Well, say thank you, if you can't say nothing else," suggested his tormentor hopefully.

"I couldn't bring nothing else," said Tommy hurriedly; "all the things was locked up. I tried to swop 'em and nearly got locked up for it. Put these on and hurry up."

The captain moistened his lips with his tongue.

"The mate'll get off directly she floats," continued Tommy. "Put these on and spoil his little game. It's raining a little now. Nobody'll see you, and as soon as you git aboard you can borrow some of the men's clothes."

"That's the ticket, cap'n," said the man. "Lord lumme, you'll 'ave everybody falling in love with you."

"Hurry up," said Tommy, dancing with impatience. "Hurry up."

The skipper, dazed and wild-eyed, stood still while his two assistants hastily dressed him, bickering somewhat about details as they did so.

"He ought to be tight-laced, I tell you," said the man.

"He can't be tight-laced without stays," said Tommy scornfully. "You ought to know that."

"Ho, can't he," said the other, discomfited. "You know too much for a young-un. Well, put a bit o' line round 'im then."

"We can't wait for a line," said Tommy, who was standing on tip-toe to tie the skipper's bonnet on. "Now tie the scarf over his chin to hide his beard, and put this veil on. It's a good job he ain't got a moustache."

The other complied, and then fell back a pace or two to gaze at his handiwork. "Strewth, though I sees it as shouldn't, you look a treat!" he remarked complacently. "Now, young-un, take 'old of his arm. Go up the back streets, and if you see anybody looking at you, call 'im Mar."

The two set off, after the man, who was a born realist, had tried to snatch a kiss from the skipper on the threshold. Fortunately for the success of the venture, it was pelting with rain, and, though a few people gazed curiously at the couple as they went hastily along, they were unmolested, and gained the wharf in safety, arriving just in time to see the schooner shoving off from the side.

At the sight the skipper held up his skirts and ran. "Ahoy!" he shouted. "Wait a minute."

The mate gave one look of blank astonishment at the extraordinary figure, and then turned away; but at that moment the stern came within jumping distance of the wharf, and uncle and nephew, moved with one impulse leaped for it and gained the deck in safety.

"Why didn't you wait when I hailed you?" demanded the skipper fiercely.

"How was I to know it was you?" inquired the mate surlily, as he realised his defeat. "I thought it was the Empress of Rooshia."

The skipper stared at him dumbly.

"An' if you take my advice," said the mate, with a sneer, "you'll keep them things on. I never see you look so well in anything afore."

"I want to borrow some o' your clothes, Bob," said the skipper, eyeing him steadily.

"Where's your own?" asked the other.

"I don't know," said the skipper. "I was took with a fit last night, Bob, and when I woke up this morning they were gone. Somebody must have took advantage of my helpless state and taken 'em."

"Very likely," said the mate, turning away to shout an order to the crew, who were busy setting sail.

"Where are they, old man?" inquired the skipper.

"How should I know?" asked the other, becoming interested in the men again.

"I mean YOUR clothes," said the skipper, who was fast losing his temper.

"Oh, mine?" said the mate. "Well, as a matter o' fact, I don't like lending my clothes. I'm rather pertickler. You might have a fit in THEM."

"You won't lend 'em to me?" asked the skipper.

"I won't," said the mate, speaking loudly, and frowning significantly at the crew, who were listening.

"Very good," said the skipper. "Ted, come here. Where's your other clothes?"

"I'm very sorry, sir," said Ted, shifting uneasily from one leg to the other, and glancing at the mate for support; "but they ain't fit for the likes of you to wear, sir." "I'm the best judge of that," said the skipper sharply. "Fetch 'em up."

"Well, to tell the truth, sir," said Ted, "I'm like the mate. I'm only a poor sailor-man, but I wouldn't lend my clothes to the Queen of England."

"You fetch up them clothes," roared the skipper snatching off his bonnet and flinging it on the deck. "Fetch 'em up at once. D'ye think I'm going about in these petticuts?"

"They're my clothes," muttered Ted doggedly.

"Very well, then, I'll have Bill's," said the skipper. "But mind you, my lad, I'll make you pay for this afore I've done with you. Bill's the only honest man aboard this ship. Gimme your hand, Bill, old man."

"I'm with them two," said Bill gruffly, as he turned away.

The skipper, biting his lips with fury, turned from one to the other, and then, with a big oath, walked forward. Before he could reach the fo'c'sle Bill and Ted dived down before him, and, by the time he had descended, sat on their chests side by side confronting him. To threats and appeals alike they turned a deaf ear, and the frantic skipper was compelled at last to go on deck again, still encumbered with the hated skirts.

"Why don't you go an' lay down," said the mate, "an' I'll send you down a nice cup o' hot tea. You'll get histericks, if you go on like that."

"I'll knock your 'ead off if you talk to me," said the skipper.

"Not you," said the mate cheerfully; "you ain't big enough. Look at that pore fellow over there."

The skipper looked in the direction indicated, and, swelling with impotent rage, shook his fist fiercely at a red-faced man with grey whiskers, who was wafting innumerable tender kisses from the bridge of a passing steamer.

"That's right," said the mate approvingly; "don't give 'im no encouragement. Love at first sight ain't worth having."

The skipper, suffering severely from suppressed emotion, went below, and the crew, after waiting a little while to make sure that he was not coming up again, made their way quietly to the mate.

"If we can only take him to Battlesea in this rig it'll be all right," said the latter. "You chaps stand by me. His slippers and sou'-wester is the only clothes he's got aboard. Chuck every needle you can lay your hands on overboard, or else he'll git trying to make a suit out of a piece of old sail or something. If we can only take him to Mr. Pearson like this, it won't be so bad after all."

While these arrangements were in hand above, the skipper and the boy were busy over others below. Various startling schemes propounded by the skipper for obtaining possession of his men's attire were rejected by the youth as unlawful, and, what was worse, impracticable. For a couple of hours they discussed ways and means, but only ended in diatribes against the mean ways of the crew; and the skipper, whose head ached still from his excesses, fell into a state of sullen despair at length, and sat silent.

"By Jove, Tommy, I've got it," he cried suddenly, starting up and hitting the table with his fist. "Where's your other suit?"

"That ain't no bigger that this one," said Tommy.

"You git it out," said the skipper, with a knowing toss of his head. "Ah, there we are. Now go in my state-room and take those off."

The wondering Tommy, who thought that great grief had turned his kinsman's brain, complied, and emerged shortly afterwards in a blanket, bringing his clothes under his arm.

"Now, do you know what I'm going to do?" inquired the skipper, with a big smile.

"No."

"Fetch me the scissors, then. Now do you know what I'm going to do?"

"Cut up the two suits and make 'em into one," hazarded the horror-stricken Tommy. "Here, stop it! Leave off!"

The skipper pushed him impatiently off, and, placing the clothes on the table, took up the scissors, and, with a few slashing strokes, cut them garments into their component parts.

"What am I to wear," said Tommy, beginning to blubber. "You didn't think of that?"

"What are you to wear, you selfish young pig?" said the skipper sternly. "Always thinking about yourself. Go and git some needles and thread, and if there's any left over, and you're a good boy, I'll see whether I can't make something for you out of the leavings."

"There ain't no needles here," whined Tommy, after a lengthened search.

"Go down the fo'c'sle and git the case of sail-makers' needles, then," said the skipper, "Don't let anyone see what you're after, an' some thread."

"Well, why couldn't you let me go in my clothes before you cut 'em up," moaned Tommy. "I don't like going up in this blanket. They'll laugh at me."

"You go at once!" thundered the skipper, and, turning his back on him, whistled softly, and began to arrange the pieces of cloth.

"Laugh away, my lads," he said cheerfully, as an uproarious burst of laughter greeted the appearance of Tommy on deck. "Wait a bit."

He waited himself for nearly twenty minutes, at the end of which time Tommy, treading on his blanket, came flying down the companion-ladder, and rolled into the cabin.

"There ain't a needle aboard the ship," he said solemnly, as he picked himself up and rubbed his head. "I've looked everywhere."

"What?" roared the skipper, hastily concealing the pieces of cloth. "Here, Ted! Ted!"

"Ay, ay, sir!" said Ted, as he came below.

"I want a sail-maker's needle," said the skipper glibly. "I've got a rent in this skirt."

"I broke the last one yesterday," said Ted, with an evil grin.

"Any other needle then," said the skipper, trying to conceal his emotion.

"I don't believe there's such a thing aboard the ship," said Ted, who had obeyed the mate's thoughtful injunction. "NOR thread. I was only saying so to the mate yesterday."

The skipper sank again to the lowest depths, waved him away, and then, getting on a corner of the locker, fell into a gloomy reverie.

"It's a pity you do things in such a hurry," said Tommy, sniffing vindictively. "You might have made sure of the needle before you spoiled my clothes. There's two of us going about ridiculous now."

The master of the Sarah Jane allowed this insolence to pass unheeded. It is in moments of deep distress that the mind of man, naturally reverting to solemn things, seeks to improve the occasion by a lecture. The skipper, chastened by suffering and disappointment, stuck his right hand in his pocket, after a lengthened search for it, and gently bidding the blanketed urchin in front of him to sit down, began:

"You see what comes of drink and cards," he said mournfully. "Instead of being at the helm of my ship, racing all the other craft down the river, I'm skulkin' down below here like—like"—

"Like an actress," suggested Tommy.

The skipper eyed him all over. Tommy, unconscious of offence, met his gaze serenely.

"If," continued the skipper, "at any time you felt like taking too much, and you stopped with the beer-mug half-way to your lips, and thought of me sitting in this disgraceful state, what would you do?"

"I dunno," replied Tommy, yawning.

"What would you do?" persisted the skipper, with great expression.

"Laugh, I s'pose," said Tommy, after a moment's thought.

The sound of a well-boxed ear rang through the cabin.

"You're an unnatural, ungrateful little toad," said the skipper fiercely. "You don't deserve to have a good, kind uncle to look after you."

"Anybody can have him for me," sobbed the indignant Tommy, as he tenderly felt his ear. "You look a precious sight more like an aunt than an uncle."

After firing this shot he vanished in a cloud of blanket, and the skipper, reluctantly abandoning a hastily-formed resolve of first flaying him alive and then flinging him overboard, sat down again and lit his pipe.

Once out of the river he came on deck again, and, ignoring by a great effort the smiles of the crew and the jibes of the mate, took command.

The only alteration he made in his dress was to substitute his sou'-wester for the bonnet, and in this guise he did his work, while the aggrieved Tommy hopped it in blankets. The three days at sea passed like a horrid dream. So covetous was his gaze, that the crew instinctively clutched their nether garments and looked to the buttoning of their coats as they passed him. He saw coats in the mainsail, and fashioned phantom trousers out of the flying jib, and towards the end began to babble of blue serges and mixed tweeds. Oblivious of fame, he had resolved to enter the harbour of Battlesea by night; but it was not to be. Near home the wind dropped, and the sun was well up before Battlesea came into view, a grey bank on the starboard bow.

Until within a mile of the harbour, the skipper held on, and then his grasp on the wheel relaxed somewhat, and he looked round anxiously for the mate.

"Where's Bob?" he shouted.

"He's very ill, sir," said Ted, shaking his head.

"Ill?" gasped the startled skipper. "Here, take the wheel a minute."

He handed it over, and grasping his skirts went hastily below. The mate was half lying, half sitting, in his bunk, groaning dismally.

"What's the matter?" inquired the skipper.

"I'm dying," said the mate. "I keep being tied up all in knots inside. I can't hold myself straight."

The other cleared his throat. "You'd better take off your clothes and lie down a bit," he said kindly. "Let me help you off with them."

"No—don't—trouble," panted the mate.

"It ain't no trouble," said the skipper, in a trembling voice.

"No, I'll keep 'em on," said the mate faintly. "I've always had an idea I'd like to die in my clothes. It may be foolish, but I can't help it."

"You'll have your wish some day, never fear, you infernal rascal," shouted the overwrought skipper. "You're shamming sickness to make me take the ship into port."

"Why shouldn't you take her in," asked the mate, with an air of innocent surprise. "It's your duty as cap'n. You'd better get above now. The bar is always shifting."

The skipper, restraining himself by a mighty effort, went on deck again, and, taking the wheel, addressed the crew. He spoke feelingly of the obedience men owed their superior officers, and the moral obligation they were under to lend them their trousers when they required them. He dwelt on the awful punishments awarded for mutiny, and proved clearly, that to allow the master of a ship to enter port in petticoats was mutiny of the worst type. He then sent them below for their clothing. They were gone such a long time that it was palpable to the meanest intellect that they did not intend to bring it. Meantime the harbour widened out before him.

There were two or three people on the quay as the Sarah Jane came within hailing distance. By the time she had passed the lantern at the end of it there were two or three dozen, and the numbers were steadily increasing at the rate of three persons for every five yards she made. Kind-hearted, humane men, anxious that their friends should not lose so great and cheap a treat, bribed small and reluctant boys with pennies to go in search of them, and by the time the schooner reached her berth, a large proportion of the population of the port was looking over each other's shoulders and shouting foolish and hilarious inquiries to the skipper. The news reached the owner, and he came hurrying down to the ship, just as the skipper, regardless of the heated remonstrances of the sightseers, was preparing to go below.

Mr. Pearson was a stout man, and he came down exploding with wrath. Then he saw the apparition, and mirth overcame him. It became necessary for three stout fellows to act as buttresses, and the more indignant the skipper looked the harder their work became. Finally he was assisted, in a weak state, and laughing hysterically, to the deck of the schooner, where he followed the skipper below, and in a voice broken with emotion demanded an explanation.

"It's the finest sight I ever saw in my life, Bross," he said when the other had finished. "I wouldn't have missed it for anything. I've been feeling very low this last week, and it's done me good. Don't talk nonsense about leaving the ship. I wouldn't lose you for anything after this, but if you like to ship a fresh mate and crew you can please yourself. If you'll only come up to the house and let Mrs. Pearson see you—she's been ailing—I'll give you a couple of pounds. Now, get your bonnet and come."

It was the mate's affair all through. He began by leaving the end of a line dangling over the stern, and the propeller, though quite unaccustomed to that sort of work, wound it up until only a few fathoms remained. It then stopped, and the mischief was not discovered until the skipper had called the engineer everything that he and the mate and three men and a boy could think of. The skipper did the interpreting through the tube which afforded the sole means of communication between the wheel and the engine-room, and the indignant engineer did the listening.

The Gem was just off Limehouse at the time, and it was evident she was going to stay there. The skipper ran her ashore and made her fast to a roomy old schooner which was lying alongside a wharf. He was then able to give a little attention to the real offender, and the unfortunate mate, who had been the most inventive of them all, realised to the full the old saying of curses coming home to roost. They brought some strangers with them, too.

"I'm going ashore," said the skipper at last. "We won't get off till next tide now. When it's low water you'll have to get down and cut the line away. A new line too! I'm ashamed o' you, Harry."

"I'm not surprised," said the engineer, who was a vindictive man.

"What do you mean by that?" demanded the mate fiercely.

"We don't want any of your bad temper," interposed the skipper severely. "NOR bad language. The men can go ashore, and the engineer too, provided he keeps steam up. But be ready for a start about five. You'll have to mind the ship."

He looked over the stern again, shook his head sadly, and, after a visit to the cabin, clambered over the schooner's side and got ashore. The men, after looking at the propeller and shaking their heads, went ashore too, and the boy, after looking at the propeller and getting ready to shake his, caught the mate's eye and omitted that part of the ceremony, from a sudden conviction that it was unhealthy.

Left alone, the mate, who was of a sensitive disposition, after a curt nod to Captain Jansell of the schooner Aquila, who had heard of the disaster, and was disposed to be sympathetically inquisitive, lit his pipe and began moodily to smoke.

When he next looked up the old man had disappeared, and a girl in a print dress and a large straw hat sat in a wicker chair reading. She was such a pretty girl that the mate forgot his troubles at once, and, after carefully putting his cap on straight, strolled casually up and down the deck.

To his mortification, the girl seemed unaware of his presence, and read steadily, occasionally looking up and chirping with a pair of ravishing lips at a blackbird, which hung in a wicker cage from the mainmast.

"That's a nice bird," said the mate, leaning against the side, and turning a look of great admiration upon it.

"Yes," said the girl, raising a pair of dark blue eyes to the bold brown ones, and taking him in at a glance.

"Does it sing?" inquired the mate, with a show of great interest.

"It does sometimes, when we are alone," was the reply.

"I should have thought the sea air would have affected its throat," said the mate, reddening. "Are you often in the London river, miss? I don't remember seeing your craft before."

"Not often," said the girl.

"You've got a fine schooner here," said the mate, eyeing it critically. "For my part, I prefer a sailer to a steamer."

"I should think you would," said the girl.

"Why?" inquired the mate tenderly, pleased at this show of interest.

"No propeller," said the girl quietly, and she left her seat and disappeared below, leaving the mate gasping painfully.

Left to himself, he became melancholy, as he realised that the great passion of his life had commenced, and would probably end within a few hours. The engineer came aboard to look at the fires, and, the steamer being now on the soft mud, good-naturedly went down and assisted him to free the propeller before going ashore again. Then he was alone once more, gazing ruefully at the bare deck of the Aquila.

It was past two o'clock in the afternoon before any signs of life other than the blackbird appeared there. Then the girl came on deck again, accompanied by a stout woman of middle age, and an appearance so affable that the mate commenced at once.

"Fine day," he said pleasantly, as he brought up in front of them.

"Lovely weather," said the mother, settling herself in her chair and putting down her work ready for a chat. "I hope the wind lasts; we start to-morrow morning's tide. You'll get off this afternoon, I s'pose."

"About five o'clock," said the mate.

"I should like to try a steamer for a change," said the mother, and waxed garrulous on sailing craft generally, and her own in particular.

"There's five of us down there, with my husband and the two boys," said she, indicating the cabin with her thumb; "naturally it gets rather stuffy."

The mate sighed. He was thinking that under some conditions there were worse things than stuffy cabins.

"And Nancy's so discontented," said the mother, looking at the girl who was reading quietly by her side. "She doesn't like ships or sailors. She gets her head turned reading those penny novelettes."

"You look after your own head," said Nancy elegantly, without looking up.

"Girls in those novels don't talk to their mothers like that," said the elder woman severely.

"They have different sorts of mothers," said Nancy, serenely turning over a page. "I hate little pokey ships and sailors smelling of tar. I never saw a sailor I liked yet."

The mate's face fell. "There's sailors and sailors," he suggested humbly.

"It's no good talking to her," said the mother, with a look of fat resignation on her face, "we can only let her go her own way; if you talked to her twenty-four hours right off it wouldn't do her any good."

"I'd like to try," said the mate, plucking up spirit.

"Would you?" said the girl, for the first time raising her head and looking him full in the face. "Impudence!"

"Perhaps you haven't seen many ships," said the impressionable mate, his eyes devouring her face. "Would you like to come and have a look at our cabin?"

"No, thanks!" said the girl sharply. Then she smiled maliciously. "I daresay mother would, though; she's fond of poking her nose into other people's business."

The mother regarded her irreverent offspring fixedly for a few moments. The mate interposed.

"I should be very pleased to show you over, ma'am," he said politely.

The mother hesitated; then she rose, and accepting the mate's assistance, clambered on to the side of the steamer, and, supported by his arms, sprang to the deck and followed him below.

"Very nice," she said, nodding approvingly, as the mate did the honours. "Very nice."

"It's nice and roomy for a little craft like ours," said the mate, as he drew a stone bottle from a locker and poured out a couple of glasses of stout. "Try a little beer, ma'am."

"What you must think o' that girl o' mine I can't think," murmured the lady, taking a modest draught.

"The young," said the mate, who had not quite reached his twenty-fifth year, "are often like that."

"It spoils her," said her mother. "She's a good-looking girl, too, in her way."

"I don't see how she can help being that," said the mate.

"Oh, get away with you," said the lady pleasantly. "She'll get fat like me as she gets older."

"She couldn't do better," said the mate tenderly.

"Nonsense," said the lady, smiling.

"You're as like as two peas," persisted the mate. "I made sure you were sisters when I saw you first."

"You ain't the first that's thought that," said the other, laughing softly; "not by a lot."

"I like to see ladies about," said the mate, who was trying desperately for a return invitation. "I wish you could always sit there. You quite brighten the cabin up."

"You're a flatterer," said his visitor, as he replenished her glass, and showed so little signs of making a move that the mate, making a pretext of seeing the engineer, hurried up on deck to singe his wings once more.

"Still reading?" he said softly, as he came abreast of the girl. "All about love, I s'pose."

"Have you left my mother down there all by herself?" inquired the girl abruptly.

"Just a minute," said the mate, somewhat crestfallen. "I just came up to see the engineer."

"Well, he isn't here," was the discouraging reply.

The mate waited a minute or two, the girl still reading quietly, and then walked back to the cabin. The sound of gentle regular breathing reached his ears, and, stepping softly, he saw to his joy that his visitor slept.

"She's asleep," said he, going back, "and she looks so comfortable I don't think I'll wake her."

"I shouldn't advise you to," said the girl; "she always wakes up cross."

"How strange we should run up against each other like this," said the mate sentimentally; "it looks like Providence, doesn't it?"

"Looks like carelessness," said the girl.

"I don't care," replied the mate. "I'm glad I did let that line go overboard. Best day's work I ever did. I shouldn't have seen you if I hadn't."

"And I don't suppose you'll ever see me again," said the girl comfortably, "so I don't see what good you've done yourself."

"I shall run down to Limehouse every time we're in port, anyway," said the mate; "it'll be odd if I don't see you sometimes. I daresay our craft'll pass each other sometimes. Perhaps in the night," he added gloomily.

"I shall sit up all night watching for you," declared Miss Jansell untruthfully.

In this cheerful fashion the conversation proceeded, the girl, who was by no means insensible to his bright eager face and well-knit figure, dividing her time in the ratio of three parts to her book and one to him. Time passed all too soon for the mate, when they were interrupted by a series of hoarse unintelligible roars proceeding from the schooner's cabin.

"That's father," said Miss Jansell, rising with a celerity which spoke well for the discipline maintained on the Aquila; "he wants me to mend his waistcoat for him."

She put down her book and left, the mate watching her until she disappeared down the companion-way. Then he sat down and waited.

One by one the crew returned to the steamer, but the schooner's deck showed no signs of life. Then the skipper came, and, having peered critically over his vessel's side, gave orders to get under way.

"If she'd only come up," said the miserable mate to himself, "I'd risk it, and ask whether I might write to her."

This chance of imperilling a promising career did not occur, however; the steamer slowly edged away from the schooner, and, picking her way between a tier of lighters, steamed slowly into clearer water.

"Full speed ahead!" roared the skipper down the tube. The engineer responded, and the mate gazed in a melancholy fashion at the water as it rapidly widened between the two vessels. Then his face brightened up suddenly as the girl ran up on deck and waved her hand. Hardly able to believe his eyes, he waved his back. The girl gesticulated violently, now pointing to the steamer, and then to the schooner.

"By Jove, that girl's taken a fancy to you," said the skipper. "She wants you to go back."

The mate sighed. "Seems like it," he said modestly.

To his astonishment the girl was now joined by her men folk, who also waved hearty farewells, and, throwing their arms about, shouted incoherently.

"Blamed if they haven't all took a fancy to you," said the puzzled skipper; "the old man's got the speaking-trumpet now. What does he say?"

"Something about life, I think," said the mate.

"They're more like jumping-jacks than anything else," said the skipper. "Just look at 'em."

The mate looked, and, as the distance increased, sprang on to the side, and, his eyes dim with emotion, waved tender farewells. If it had not been for the presence of the skipper—a tremendous stickler for decorum—he would have kissed his hand.

It was not until Gravesend was passed, and the side-lights of the shipping were trying to show in the gathering dusk, that he awoke from his tender apathy. It is probable that it would have lasted longer than that but for a sudden wail of anguish and terror which proceeded from the cabin and rang out on the still warm air.

"Sakes alive!" said the skipper, starting; "what's that?"

Before the mate could reply, the companion was pushed back, and a middle-aged woman, labouring under strong excitement, appeared on deck.

"You villain!" she screamed excitably, rushing up to the mate. "Take me back; take me back!"

"What's all this, Harry?" demanded the skipper sternly.

"He—he—he—asked me to go into the cab—cabin," sobbed Mrs. Jansell, "and sent me to sleep, and too—too—took me away. My husband'll kill me; I know he will. Take me back."

"What do you want to be took back to be killed for?" interposed one of the men judicially.

"I might ha' known what he meant when he said I brightened the cabin up," said Mrs. Jansell; "and when he said he thought me and my daughter were sisters. He said he'd like me to sit there always, the wretch!"

"Did you say that?" inquired the skipper fiercely.

"Well, I did," said the miserable mate; "but I didn't mean her to take it that way. She went to sleep, and I forgot all about her."

"What did you say such silly lies for, then?" demanded the skipper.

The mate hung his head.

"Old enough to be your mother too," said the skipper severely. "Here's a nice thing to happen aboard my ship, and afore the boy too!"

"Blast the boy!" said the goaded mate.

"Take me back," wailed Mrs. Jansell; "you don't know how jealous my husband is."

"He won't hurt you," said the skipper kindly "he won't be jealous of a woman your time o' life; that is, not if he's got any sense. You'll have to go as far as Boston with us now. I've lost too much time already to go back."

"You must take me back," said Mrs. Jansell passionately.

"I'm not going back for anybody," said the skipper. "But you can make your mind quite easy: you're as safe aboard my ship as what you would be alone on a raft in the middle of the Atlantic; and as for the mate, he was only chaffing you. Wasn't you, Harry?"

The mate made some reply, but neither Mrs. Jansell, the skipper, nor the men, who were all listening eagerly, caught it, and his unfortunate victim, accepting the inevitable, walked to the side of the ship and gazed disconsolately astern.

It was not until the following morning that the mate, who had received orders to mess for'ard, saw her, and ignoring the fact that everybody suspended work to listen, walked up and bade her good morning.

"Harry," said the skipper warningly.

"All right," said the mate shortly. "I want to speak to you very particularly," he said nervously, and led his listener aft, followed by three of the crew who came to clean the brasswork, and who listened mutinously when they were ordered to defer unwonted industry to a more fitting time. The deck clear, the mate began, and in a long rambling statement, which Mrs. Jansell at first thought the ravings of lunacy, acquainted her with the real state of his feelings.

"I never did!" said she, when he had finished. "Never! Why, you hadn't seen her before yesterday."

"Of course I shall take you back by train," said the mate, "and tell your husband how sorry I am."

"I might have suspected something when you said all those nice things to me," said the mollified lady. "Well, you must take your chance, like all the rest of them. She can only say 'No,' again. It'll explain this affair better, that's one thing; but I expect they'll laugh at you."

"I don't care," said the mate stoutly. "You're on my side, ain't you?"

Mrs. Jansell laughed, and the mate, having succeeded beyond his hopes in the establishment of amicable relations, went about his duties with a light heart.

By the time they reached Boston the morning was far advanced, and after the Gem was comfortably berthed he obtained permission of the skipper to accompany the fair passenger to London, beguiling the long railway journey by every means in his power. Despite his efforts, however, the journey began to pall upon his companion, and it was not until evening was well advanced that they found themselves in the narrow streets of Limehouse.

"We'll see how the land lies first," said he, as they approached the wharf and made their way cautiously on to the quay.

The Aquila was still alongside, and the mate's heart thumped violently as he saw the cause of all the trouble sitting alone on the deck. She rose with a little start as her mother stepped carefully aboard, and, running to her, kissed her affectionately, and sat her down on the hatches.

"Poor mother," she said caressingly. "What did you bring that lunatic back with you for?"

"He would come," said Mrs. Jansell. "Hush! here comes your father."

The master of the Aquila came on deck as she spoke, and walking slowly up to the group, stood sternly regarding them. Under his gaze the mate breathlessly reeled off his tale, noticing with somewhat mixed feelings the widening grin of his listener as he proceeded.

"Well, you're a lively sort o' man," said the skipper as he finished. "In one day you tie up your own ship, run off with my wife, and lose us a tide. Are you always like that?"

"I want somebody to look after me, I s'pose," said the mate, with a side glance at Nancy.

"Well, we'd put you up for the night," said the skipper, with his arm round his wife's shoulders; "but you're such a chap. I'm afraid you'd burn the ship down, or something. What do you think, old girl?"

"I think we'll try him this once," said his wife. "And now I'll go down and see about supper; I want it."

The old couple went below, and the young one remained on deck. Nancy went and leaned against the side; and as she appeared to have quite forgotten his presence, the mate, after some hesitation, joined her.

"Hadn't you better go down and get some supper?" she asked.

"I'd sooner stay here, if yon don't mind," said the mate. "I like watching the lights going up and down; I could stay here for hours."

"I'll leave you, then," said the girl; "I'm hungry."

She tripped lightly off with a smothered laugh, leaving the fairly-trapped man gazing indignantly at the lights which had lured him to destruction.

From below he heard the cheerful clatter of crockery, accompanied by a savoury incense, and talk and laughter. He imagined the girl making fun of his sentimental reasons for staying on deck; but, too proud to meet her ironical glances, stayed doggedly where he was, resolving to be off by the first train in the morning. He was roused from his gloom by a slight touch on his arm, and, turning sharply, saw the girl by his side.

"Supper's quite ready," said she soberly. "And if you want to admire the lights very much, come up and see them when I do—after supper."

IN MID-ATLANTIC

"No, sir," said the night-watchman, as he took a seat on a post at the end of the jetty, and stowed a huge piece of tobacco in his cheek. "No, man an' boy, I was at sea forty years afore I took on this job, but I can't say as ever I saw a real, downright ghost."

This was disappointing, and I said so. Previous experience of the power of Bill's vision had led me to expect something very different.

"Not but what I've known some queer things happen," said Bill, fixing his eyes on the Surrey side, and going off into a kind of trance. "Queer things."

I waited patiently; Bill's eyes, after resting for some time on Surrey, began to slowly cross the river, paused midway in reasonable hopes of a collision between a tug with its flotilla of barges and a penny steamer, and then came back to me.

"You heard that yarn old Cap'n Harris was telling the other day about the skipper he knew having a warning one night to alter his course, an' doing so, picked up five live men and three dead skeletons in a open boat?" he inquired.

I nodded.

"The yarn in various forms is an old one," said I.

"It's all founded on something I told him once," said Bill. "I don't wish to accuse Cap'n Harris of taking another man's true story an' spoiling it; he's got a bad memory, that's all. Fust of all, he forgets he ever heard the yarn; secondly, he goes and spoils it."

I gave a sympathetic murmur. Harris was as truthful an old man as ever breathed, but his tales were terribly restricted by this circumstance, whereas Bill's were limited by nothing but his own imagination.

"It was about fifteen years ago now," began Bill, getting the quid into a bye-way of his cheek, where it would not impede his utterance "I was A. B. on the Swallow, a barque, trading wherever we could pick up stuff. On this v'y'ge we was bound from London to Jamaica with a general cargo.

"The start of that v'y'ge was excellent. We was towed out of the St. Katherine's Docks here, to the Nore, an' the tug left us to a stiff breeze, which fairly raced us down Channel and out into the Atlantic. Everybody was saying what a fine v'y'ge we was having, an' what quick time we should make, an' the fust mate was in such a lovely temper that you might do anything with him a'most.

"We was about ten days out, an' still slipping along in this spanking way, when all of a sudden things changed. I was at the wheel with the second mate one night, when the skipper, whose name was Brown, came up from below in a uneasy sort o' fashion, and stood looking at us for some time without speaking. Then at last he sort o' makes up his mind, and ses he—

"'Mr. McMillan, I've just had a most remarkable experience, an' I don't know what to do about it.'

"'Yes, sir?' ses Mr. McMillan.

"'Three times I Ve been woke up this night by something shouting in my ear, "Steer nor'-nor'-west!"' ses the cap'n very solemnly, '"Steer nor'-nor'-west!" that's all it says. The first time I thought it was somebody got into my cabin skylarking, and I laid for 'em with a stick but I've heard it three times, an' there's nothing there.'

"'It's a supernatural warning,' ses the second mate, who had a great uncle once who had the second sight, and was the most unpopular man of his family, because he always knew what to expect, and laid his plans according.

"'That's what I think,' ses the cap'n. 'There's some poor shipwrecked fellow creatures in distress."

"'It's a verra grave responsebeelity,' ses Mr. McMillan 'I should just ca' up the fairst mate.'

"'Bill,' ses the cap'n, 'just go down below, and tell Mr. Salmon I'd like a few words with him partikler.'

"Well, I went down below, and called up the first mate, and as soon as I'd explained to him what he was wanted for, he went right off into a fit of outrageous bad language, an' hit me. He came right up on deck in his pants an' socks. A most disrespekful way to come to the cap'n, but he was that hot and excited he didn't care what he did.

"'Mr. Salmon,' ses the cap'n gravely, 'I've just had a most solemn warning, and I want to—'

"'I know,' says the mate gruffly.

"'What! have you heard it too?' ses the cap'n, in surprise. 'Three times?' "I heard it from him,' ses the mate, pointing to me. 'Nightmare, sir, nightmare.'

"'It was not nightmare, sir,' ses the cap'n, very huffy, 'an if I hear it again, I 'm going to alter this ship's course.'

"Well, the fust mate was in a hole. He wanted to call the skipper something which he knew wasn't discipline. I knew what it was, an' I knew if the mate didn't do something he'd be ill, he was that sort of man, everything flew to his head. He walked away, and put his head over the side for a bit, an' at last, when he came back, he was, comparatively speaking, calm.

"'You mustn't hear them words again, sir,' ses he; 'don't go to sleep again to-night. Stay up, an' we'll have a hand o' cards, and in the morning you take a good stiff dose o' rhoobarb. Don't spoil one o' the best trips we've ever had for the sake of a pennyworth of rhoobarb,' ses he, pleading-like.

"'Mr. Salmon,' ses the cap'n, very angry, 'I shall not fly in the face o' Providence in any such way. I shall sleep as usual, an' as for your rhoobarb,' ses the cap'n, working hisself up into a passion— 'damme, sir, I'll—I'll dose the whole crew with it, from first mate to cabin-boy, if I have any impertinence.'

"Well, Mr. Salmon, who was getting very mad, stalks down below, followed by the cap'n, an' Mr. McMillan was that excited that he even started talking to me about it. Half-an-hour arterwards the cap'n comes running up on deck again.

"'Mr. McMillan,' ses he excitedly, 'steer nor'-nor'-west until further orders. I've heard it again, an' this time it nearly split the drum of my ear.'

"The ship's course was altered, an' after the old man was satisfied he went back to bed again, an' almost directly arter eight bells went, an' I was relieved. I wasn't on deck when the fust mate come up, but those that were said he took it very calm. He didn't say a word. He just sat down on the poop, and blew his cheeks out.

"As soon as ever it was daylight the skipper was on deck with his glasses. He sent men up to the masthead to keep a good look-out, an' he was dancing about like a cat on hot bricks all the morning.

"'How long are we to go on this course, sir?' asks Mr. Salmon, about ten o'clock in the morning.

"'I've not made up my mind, sir,' ses the cap'n, very stately; but I could see he was looking a trifle foolish.

"At twelve o'clock in the day, the fust mate got a cough, and every time he coughed it seemed to act upon the skipper, and make him madder and madder. Now that it was broad daylight, Mr. McMillan didn't seem to be so creepy as the night before, an' I could see the cap'n was only waiting for the slightest excuse to get into our proper course again.

"'That's a nasty, bad cough o' yours, Mr. Salmon,' ses he, eyeing the mate very hard.

"'Yes, a nasty, irritating sort o' cough, sir,' ses the other; 'it worries me a great deal. It's this going up nor'ards what's sticking in my throat,' ses he.

"The cap'n give a gulp, and walked off, but he comes back in a minute, and ses he—

"'Mr. Salmon, I should think it a great pity to lose a valuable officer like yourself, even to do good to others. There's a hard ring about that cough I don't like, an' if you really think it's going up this bit north, why, I don't mind putting the ship in her course again.'

"Well, the mate thanked him kindly, and he was just about to give the orders when one o' the men who was at the masthead suddenly shouts out—

"'Ahoy! Small boat on the port bow!'

"The cap'n started as if he'd been shot, and ran up the rigging with his glasses. He came down again almost direckly, and his face was all in a glow with pleasure and excitement.

"'Mr. Salmon,' ses he, 'here's a small boat with a lug sail in the middle o' the Atlantic, with one pore man lying in the bottom of her. What do you think o' my warning now?'

"The mate didn't say anything at first, but he took the glasses and had a look, an' when he came back anyone could see his opinion of the skipper had gone up miles and miles.

"'It's a wonderful thing, sir,' ses he, 'and one I'll remember all my life. It's evident that you've been picked out as a instrument to do this good work.'

"I'd never heard the fust mate talk like that afore, 'cept once when he fell overboard, when he was full, and stuck in the Thames mud. He said it was Providence; though, as it was low water, according to the tide-table, I couldn't see what Providence had to do with it myself. He was as excited as anybody, and took the wheel himself, and put the ship's head for the boat, and as she came closer, our boat was slung out, and me and the second mate and three other men dropped into her, an' pulled so as to meet the other.

"'Never mind the boat; we don't want to be bothered with her,' shouts out the cap'n as we pulled away—'Save the man!'

"I'll say this for Mr. McMillan, he steered that boat beautifully, and we ran alongside o' the other as clever as possible. Two of us shipped our oars, and gripped her tight, and then we saw that she was just an ordinary boat, partly decked in, with the head and shoulders of a man showing in the opening, fast asleep, and snoring like thunder.

"'Puir chap,' ses Mr. McMillan, standing up. 'Look how wasted he is.'

"He laid hold o' the man by the neck of his coat an' his belt, an', being a very powerful man, dragged him up and swung him into our boat, which was bobbing up and down, and grating against the side of the other. We let go then, an' the man we'd rescued opened his eyes as Mr. McMillan tumbled over one of the thwarts with him, and, letting off a roar like a bull, tried to jump back into his boat.

"'Hold him!' shouted the second mate. 'Hold him tight! He's mad, puir feller.'

"By the way that man fought and yelled, we thought the mate was right, too. He was a short, stiff chap, hard as iron, and he bit and kicked and swore for all he was worth, until at last we tripped him up and tumbled him into the bottom of the boat, and held him there with his head hanging back over a thwart.

"'It's all right, my puir feller,' ses the second mate; 'ye're in good hands—ye're saved.'

"'Damme!' ses the man; 'what's your little game? Where's my boat—eh? Where's my boat?'

"He wriggled a bit, and got his head up, and, when he saw it bowling along two or three hundred yards away, his temper got the better of him, and he swore that if Mr. McMillan didn't row after it he'd knife him.

"'We can't bother about the boat,' ses the mate; 'we've had enough bother to rescue you.'

"'Who the devil wanted you to rescue me?' bellowed the man. 'I'll make you pay for this, you miserable swabs. If there's any law in Amurrica, you shall have it!'

"By this time we had got to the ship, which had shortened sail, and the cap'n was standing by the side, looking down upon the stranger with a big, kind smile which nearly sent him crazy.

"'Welcome aboard, my pore feller,' ses he, holding out his hand as the chap got up the side.

"'Are you the author of this outrage?' ses the man fiercely. "'I don't understand you,' ses the cap'n, very dignified, and drawing himself up.

"'Did you send your chaps to sneak me out o' my boat while I was having forty winks?' roars the other. 'Damme! that's English, ain't it?'

"'Surely,' ses the cap'n, 'surely you didn't wish to be left to perish in that little craft. I had a supernatural warning to steer this course on purpose to pick you up, and this is your gratitude.'

"'Look here!' ses the other. 'My name's Cap'n Naskett, and I'm doing a record trip from New York to Liverpool in the smallest boat that has ever crossed the Atlantic, an' you go an' bust everything with your cussed officiousness. If you think I'm going to be kidnapped just to fulfil your beastly warnings, you've made a mistake. I'll have the law on you, that's what I'll do. Kidnapping's a punishable offence.'

"'What did you come here for, then?' ses the cap'n.

"'Come!' howls Cap'n Naskett. 'Come! A feller sneaks up alongside o' me with a boat-load of street-sweepings dressed as sailors, and snaps me up while I'm asleep, and you ask me what I come for. Look here. You clap on all sail and catch that boat o' mine, and put me back, and I'll call it quits. If you don't, I'll bring a law-suit agin you, and make you the laughing-stock of two continents into the bargain.'

"Well, to make the best of a bad bargain, the cap'n sailed after the cussed little boat, and Mr. Salmon, who thought more than enough time had been lost already, fell foul o' Cap'n Naskett. They was both pretty talkers, and the way they went on was a education for every sailorman afloat. Every man aboard got as near as they durst to listen to them; but I must say Cap'n Naskett had the best of it. He was a sarkastik man, and pretended to think the ship was fitted out just to pick up shipwrecked people, an' he also pretended to think we was castaways what had been saved by it. He said o' course anybody could see at a glance we wasn't sailormen, an' he supposed Mr. Salmon was a butcher what had been carried out to sea while paddling at Margate to strengthen his ankles. He said a lot more of this sort of thing, and all this time we was chasing his miserable little boat, an' he was admiring the way she sailed, while the fust mate was answering his reflexshuns, an' I'm sure that not even our skipper was more pleased than Mr. Salmon when we caught it at last, and shoved him back. He was ungrateful up to the last, an', just before leaving the ship, actually went up to Cap'n Brown, and advised him to shut his eyes an' turn round three times and catch what he could.

"I never saw the skipper so upset afore, but I heard him tell Mr. McMillan that night that if he ever went out of his way again after a craft, it would only be to run it down. Most people keep pretty quiet about supernatural things that happen to them, but he was about the quietest I ever heard of, an', what's more, he made everyone else keep quiet about it, too. Even when he had to steer nor'-

nor'-west arter that in the way o' business he didn't like it, an' he was about the most cruelly disappointed man you ever saw when he heard afterwards that Cap'n Naskett got safe to Liverpool."

IN THE FAMILY

The oldest inhabitant of Claybury sat beneath the sign of the "Cauliflower" and gazed with affectionate, but dim, old eyes in the direction of the village street.

"No; Claybury men ain't never been much of ones for emigrating," he said, turning to the youthful traveller who was resting in the shade with a mug of ale and a cigarette. "They know they'd 'ave to go a long way afore they'd find a place as 'ud come up to this."

He finished the tablespoonful of beer in his mug and sat for so long with his head back and the inverted vessel on his face that the traveller, who at first thought it was the beginning of a conjuring trick, colored furiously, and asked permission to refill it.

Now and then a Claybury man has gone to foreign parts, said the old man, drinking from the replenished mug, and placing it where the traveller could mark progress without undue strain; but they've, generally speaking, come back and wished as they'd never gone.

The on'y man as I ever heard of that made his fortune by emigrating was Henery Walker's great-uncle, Josiah Walker by name, and he wasn't a Claybury man at all. He made his fortune out o' sheep in Australey, and he was so rich and well-to-do that he could never find time to answer the letters that Henery Walker used to send him when he was hard up.

Henery Walker used to hear of 'im through a relation of his up in London, and tell us all about 'im and his money up at this here "Cauliflower" public-house. And he used to sit and drink his beer and wonder who would 'ave the old man's money arter he was dead.

When the relation in London died Henery Walker left off hearing about his uncle, and he got so worried over thinking that the old man might die and leave his money to strangers that he got quite thin. He talked of emigrating to Australey 'imself, and then, acting on the advice of Bill Chambers—who said it was a cheaper thing to do—he wrote to his uncle instead, and, arter reminding 'im that 'e was an old man living in a strange country, 'e asked 'im to come to Claybury and make his 'ome with 'is loving grand-nephew.

It was a good letter, because more than one gave 'im a hand with it, and there was little bits o' Scripture in it to make it more solemn-like. It was wrote on pink paper with pie-crust edges and put in a green envelope, and Bill Chambers said a man must 'ave a 'art of stone if that didn't touch it.

Four months arterwards Henery Walker got an answer to 'is letter from 'is great-uncle. It was a nice letter, and, arter thanking Henery Walker for all his kindness, 'is uncle said that he was getting an old man, and p'r'aps he should come and lay 'is bones in England arter all, and if he did 'e should certainly come and see his grand-nephew, Henery Walker.

Most of us thought Henery Walker's fortune was as good as made, but Bob Pretty, a nasty, low poaching chap that has done wot he could to give Claybury a bad name, turned up his nose at it.

"I'll believe he's coming 'ome when I see him," he ses. "It's my belief he went to Australey to get out o' your way, Henery."

"As it 'appened he went there afore I was born," ses Henery Walker, firing up.

"He knew your father," ses Bob Pretty, "and he didn't want to take no risks."

They 'ad words then, and arter that every time Bob Pretty met 'im he asked arter his great-uncle's 'ealth, and used to pretend to think 'e was living with 'im.

"You ought to get the old gentleman out a bit more, Henery," he would say; "it can't be good for 'im to be shut up in the 'ouse so much—especially your 'ouse."

Henery Walker used to get that riled he didn't know wot to do with 'imself, and as time went on, and he began to be afraid that 'is uncle never would come back to England, he used to get quite nasty if anybody on'y so much as used the word "uncle" in 'is company.

It was over six months since he 'ad had the letter from 'is uncle, and 'e was up here at the "Cauliflower" with some more of us one night, when Dicky Weed, the tailor, turns to Bob Pretty and he ses, "Who's the old gentleman that's staying with you, Bob?"

Bob Pretty puts down 'is beer very careful and turns round on 'im.

"Old gentleman?" he ses, very slow. "Wot are you talking about?"

"I mean the little old gentleman with white whiskers and a squeaky voice," ses Dicky Weed.

"You've been dreaming," ses Bob, taking up 'is beer ag'in.

"I see 'im too, Bob," ses Bill Chambers.

"Ho, you did, did you?" ses Bob Pretty, putting down 'is mug with a bang. "And wot d'ye mean by coming spying round my place, eh? Wot d'ye mean by it?"

"Spying?" ses Bill Chambers, gaping at 'im with 'is mouth open; "I wasn't spying. Anyone 'ud think you 'ad done something you was ashamed of."

"You mind your business and I'll mind mine," ses Bob, very fierce.

"I was passing the 'ouse," ses Bill Chambers, looking round at us, "and I see an old man's face at the bedroom winder, and while I was wondering who 'e was a hand come and drawed 'im away. I see 'im as plain as ever I see anything in my life, and the hand, too. Big and dirty it was."

"And he's got a cough," ses Dicky Weed—"a churchyard cough—I 'eard it."

"It ain't much you don't hear, Dicky," ses Bob Pretty, turning on 'im; "the on'y thing you never did 'ear, and never will 'ear, is any good of yourself."

He kicked over a chair wot was in 'is way and went off in such a temper as we'd never seen 'im in afore, and, wot was more surprising still, but I know it's true, 'cos I drunk it up myself, he'd left over arf a pint o' beer in 'is mug.

"He's up to something," ses Sam Jones, starting arter him; "mark my words."

We couldn't make head nor tail out of it, but for some days arterward you'd ha' thought that Bob Pretty's 'ouse was a peep-show. Everybody stared at the winders as they went by, and the children played in front of the 'ouse and stared in all day long. Then the old gentleman was seen one day as bold as brass sitting at the winder, and we heard that it was a pore old tramp Bob Pretty 'ad met on the road and given a home to, and he didn't like 'is good-'artedness to be known for fear he should be made fun of.

Nobody believed that, o' course, and things got more puzzling than ever. Once or twice the old gentleman went out for a walk, but Bob Pretty or 'is missis was always with 'im, and if anybody tried to speak to him they always said 'e was deaf and took 'im off as fast as they could. Then one night up at the "Cauliflower" here Dicky Weed came rushing in with a bit o' news that took everybody's breath away.

"I've just come from the post-office," he ses, "and there's a letter for Bob Pretty's old gentleman! Wot d'ye think o' that?"

"If you could tell us wot's inside it you might 'ave something to brag about," ses Henery Walker.

"I don't want to see the inside," ses Dicky Weed; "the name on the outside was good enough for me. I couldn't hardly believe my own eyes, but there it was: 'Mr. Josiah Walker,' as plain as the nose on your face."

O' course, we see it all then, and wondered why we hadn't thought of it afore; and we stood quiet listening to the things that Henery Walker said about a man that would go and steal another man's great-uncle from 'im. Three times Smith, the landlord, said, "Hush!" and the fourth time he put Henery Walker outside and told 'im to stay there till he 'ad lost his voice.

Henery Walker stayed outside five minutes, and then 'e come back in ag'in to ask for advice. His idea seemed to be that, as the old gentleman was deaf, Bob Pretty was passing 'isself off as Henery Walker, and the disgrace was a'most more than 'e could bear. He began to get excited ag'in, and Smith 'ad just said "Hush!" once more when we 'eard somebody whistling outside, and in come Bob Pretty.

He 'ad hardly got 'is face in at the door afore Henery Walker started on 'im, and Bob Pretty stood there, struck all of a heap, and staring at 'im as though he couldn't believe his ears.

"'Ave you gone mad, Henery?" he ses, at last.

"Give me back my great-uncle," ses Henery Walker, at the top of 'is voice.

Bob Pretty shook his 'ead at him. "I haven't got your great-uncle, Henery," he ses, very gentle. "I know the name is the same, but wot of it? There's more than one Josiah Walker in the world. This one is no relation to you at all; he's a very respectable old gentleman."

"I'll go and ask 'im," ses Henery Walker, getting up, "and I'll tell 'im wot sort o' man you are, Bob Pretty."

"He's gone to bed now, Henery," ses Bob Pretty.

"I'll come in the fust thing to-morrow morning, then," ses Henery Walker.

"Not in my 'ouse, Henery," ses Bob Pretty; "not arter the things you've been sayin' about me. I'm a pore man, but I've got my pride. Besides, I tell you he ain't your uncle. He's a pore old man I'm giving a 'ome to, and I won't 'ave 'im worried."

"'Ow much does 'e pay you a week, Bob?" ses Bill Chambers.

Bob Pretty pretended not to hear 'im.

"Where did your wife get the money to buy that bonnet she 'ad on on Sunday?" ses Bill Chambers. "My wife ses it's the fust new bonnet she has 'ad since she was married."

"And where did the new winder curtains come from?" ses Peter Gubbins.

Bob Pretty drank up 'is beer and stood looking at them very thoughtful; then he opened the door and went out without saying a word.

"He's got your great-uncle a prisoner in his 'ouse, Henery," ses Bill Chambers; "it's easy for to see that the pore old gentleman is getting past things, and I shouldn't wonder if Bob Pretty don't make 'im leave all 'is money to 'im."

Henery Walker started raving ag'in, and for the next few days he tried his 'ardest to get a few words with 'is great-uncle, but Bob Pretty was too much for 'im. Everybody in Claybury said wot a shame it was, but it was all no good, and Henery Walker used to leave 'is work and stand outside Bob Pretty's for hours at a time in the 'opes of getting a word with the old man.

He got 'is chance at last, in quite an unexpected way. We was up 'ere at the "Cauliflower" one evening, and, as it 'appened, we was talking about Henery Walker's great-uncle, when the door opened, and who should walk in but the old gentleman 'imself. Everybody left off talking and stared at 'im, but he walked up to the bar and ordered a glass o' gin and beer as comfortable as you please.

Bill Chambers was the fust to get 'is presence of mind back, and he set off arter Henery Walker as fast as 'is legs could carry 'im, and in a wunnerful short time, considering, he came back with Henery, both of 'em puffing and blowing their 'ardest.

"There—he—is!" ses Bill Chambers, pointing to the old gentleman.

Henery Walker gave one look, and then 'e slipped over to the old man and stood all of a tremble, smiling at 'im. "Good-evening," he ses.

"Wot?" ses the old gentleman.

"Good-evening!" ses Henery Walker ag'in.

"I'm a bit deaf," ses the old gentleman, putting his 'and to his ear.

"GOOD-EVENING!" ses Henery Walker ag'in, shouting. "I'm your grand-nephew, Henery Walker!"

"Ho, are you?" ses the old gentleman, not at all surprised. "Bob Pretty was telling me all about you."

"I 'ope you didn't listen to 'im," ses Henery Walker, all of a tremble. "Bob Pretty'd say anything except his prayers."

"He ses you're arter my money," ses the old gentleman, looking at 'im.

"He's a liar, then," ses Henery Walker; "he's arter it 'imself. And it ain't a respectable place for you to stay at. Anybody'll tell you wot a rascal Bob Pretty is. Why, he's a byword."

"Everybody is arter my money," ses the old gentleman, looking round. "Everybody."

"I 'ope you'll know me better afore you've done with me, uncle," ses Henery Walker, taking a seat alongside of Mm. "Will you 'ave another mug o' beer?"

"Gin and beer," ses the old gentleman, cocking his eye up very fierce at Smith, the landlord; "and mind the gin don't get out ag'in, same as it did in the last."

Smith asked 'im wot he meant, but 'is deafness come on ag'in. Henery Walker 'ad an extra dose o' gin put in, and arter he 'ad tasted it the old gentleman seemed to get more amiable-like, and 'im and Henery Walker sat by theirselves talking quite comfortable.

"Why not come and stay with me?" ses Henery Walker, at last. "You can do as you please and have the best of everything."

"Bob Pretty ses you're arter my money," ses the old gentleman, shaking his 'ead. "I couldn't trust you."

"He ses that to put you ag'in me," ses Henery Walker, pleading-like.

"Well, wot do you want me to come and live with you for, then?" ses old Mr. Walker.

"Because you're my great-uncle," ses Henery Walker, "and my 'ouse is the proper place for you. Blood is thicker than water."

"And you don't want my money?" ses the old man, looking at 'im very sharp.

"Certainly not," ses Henery Walker.

"And 'ow much 'ave I got to pay a week?" ses old Mr. Walker. "That's the question?"

"Pay?" ses Henery Walker, speaking afore he 'ad time to think. "Pay? Why, I don't want you to pay anything."

The old gentleman said as 'ow he'd think it over, and Henery started to talk to 'im about his father and an old aunt named Maria, but 'e stopped 'im sharp, and said he was sick and tired of the whole Walker family, and didn't want to 'ear their names ag'in as long as he lived. Henery Walker began to talk about Australey then, and asked 'im 'ow many sheep he'd got, and the words was 'ardly out of 'is mouth afore the old gentleman stood up and said he was arter his money ag'in.

Henery Walker at once gave 'im some more gin and beer, and arter he 'ad drunk it the old gentleman said that he'd go and live with 'im for a little while to see 'ow he liked it.

"But I sha'n't pay anything," he ses, very sharp; "mind that."

"I wouldn't take it if you offered it to me," ses Henery Walker. "You'll come straight 'ome with me to-night, won't you?"

Afore old Mr. Walker could answer the door opened and in came Bob Pretty. He gave one look at Henery Walker and then he walked straight over to the old gentleman and put his 'and on his shoulder.

"Why, I've been looking for you everywhere, Mr. Walker," he ses. "I couldn't think wot had 'appened to you."

"You needn't worry yourself, Bob," ses Henery Walker; "he's coming to live with me now."

"Don't you believe it," ses Bob Pretty, taking hold of old Mr. Walker by the arm; "he's my lodger, and he's coming with me."

He began to lead the old gentleman towards the door, but Henery Walker, wot was still sitting down, threw 'is arms round his legs and held 'im tight. Bob Pretty pulled one way and Henery Walker pulled the other, and both of 'em shouted to each other to leave go. The row they made was awful, but old Mr. Walker made more noise than the two of 'em put together.

"You leave go o' my lodger," ses Bob Pretty.

"You leave go o' my great-uncle—my dear great-uncle," ses Henery Walker, as the old gentleman called 'im a bad name and asked 'im whether he thought he was made of iron.

I believe they'd ha' been at it till closing-time, on'y Smith, the landlord, came running in from the back and told them to go outside. He 'ad to shout to make 'imself heard, and all four of 'em seemed to be trying which could make the most noise.

"He's my lodger," ses Bob Pretty, "and he can't go without giving me proper notice; that's the lor—a week's notice."

They all shouted ag'in then, and at last the old gentleman told Henery Walker to give Bob Pretty ten shillings for the week's notice and ha' done with 'im. Henery Walker 'ad only got four shillings with 'im, but 'e borrowed the rest from Smith, and arter he 'ad told Bob Pretty wot he thought of 'im he took old Mr. Walker by the arm and led him 'ome a'most dancing for joy.

Mrs. Walker was nearly as pleased as wot 'e was, and the fuss they made of the old gentleman was sinful a'most. He 'ad to speak about it 'imself at last, and he told 'em plain that when 'e wanted arf-a-dozen sore-eyed children to be brought down in their night-gowns to kiss 'im while he was eating sausages, he'd say so.

Arter that Mrs. Walker was afraid that 'e might object when her and her 'usband gave up their bedroom to 'im; but he didn't. He took it all as 'is right, and when Henery Walker, who was sleeping in the next room with three of 'is boys, fell out o' bed for the second time, he got up and rapped on the wall.

Bob Pretty came round the next morning with a tin box that belonged to the old man, and 'e was so perlite and nice to 'im that Henery Walker could see that he 'ad 'opes of getting 'im back ag'in. The box was carried upstairs and put under old Mr. Walker's bed, and 'e was so partikler about its being locked, and about nobody being about when 'e opened it, that Mrs. Walker went arf out of her mind with curiosity.

"I s'pose you've looked to see that Bob Pretty didn't take anything out of it?" ses Henery Walker.

"He didn't 'ave the chance," ses the old gentleman. "It's always kep' locked."

"It's a box that looks as though it might 'ave been made in Australey," ses Henery Walker, who was longing to talk about them parts.

"If you say another word about Australey to me," ses old Mr. Walker, firing up, "off I go. Mind that! You're arter my money, and if you're not careful you sha'n't 'ave a farthing of it."

That was the last time the word "Australey" passed Henery Walker's lips, and even when 'e saw his great-uncle writing letters there he didn't say anything. And the old man was so suspicious of Mrs. Walker's curiosity that all the letters that was wrote to 'im he 'ad sent to Bob Pretty's. He used to call there pretty near every morning to see whether any 'ad come for 'im.

In three months Henery Walker 'adn't seen the color of 'is money once, and, wot was worse still, he took to giving Henery's things away. Mrs. Walker 'ad been complaining for some time of 'ow bad the hens had been laying, and one morning at breakfast-time she told her 'usband that, besides missing eggs, two of 'er best hens 'ad been stolen in the night.

"They wasn't stolen," ses old Mr. Walker, putting down 'is teacup. "I took 'em round this morning and give 'em to Bob Pretty."

"Give 'em to Bob Pretty?" ses Henery Walker, arf choking. "Wot for?"

"'Cos he asked me for 'em," ses the old gentleman. "Wot are you looking at me like that for?"

Henery couldn't answer 'im, and the old gentleman, looking very fierce, got up from the table and told Mrs. Walker to give 'im his hat. Henery Walker clung to 'im with tears in his eyes a'most and begged 'im not to go, and arter a lot of talk old Mr. Walker said he'd look over it this time, but it mustn't occur ag'in.

Arter that 'e did as 'e liked with Henery Walker's things, and Henery dursen't say a word to 'im. Bob Pretty used to come up and flatter 'im and beg 'im to go back and lodge with 'im, and Henery was so afraid he'd go that he didn't say a word when old Mr. Walker used to give Bob Pretty things to make up for 'is disappointment. He 'eard on the quiet from Bill Chambers, who said that the old man 'ad told it to Bob Pretty as a dead secret, that 'e 'ad left 'im all his money, and he was ready to put up with anything.

The old man must ha' been living with Henery Walker for over eighteen months when one night he passed away in 'is sleep. Henery knew that his 'art was wrong, because he 'ad just paid Dr. Green 'is bill for saying that 'e couldn't do anything for 'im, but it was a surprise to 'im all the same. He blew his nose 'ard and Mrs. Walker kept rubbing 'er eyes with her apron while they talked in whispers and wondered 'ow much money they 'ad come in for.

In less than ten minutes the news was all over Claybury, and arf the people in the place hanging round in front of the 'ouse waiting to hear 'ow much the Walkers 'ad come in for. Henery Walker pulled the blind on one side for a moment and shook his 'ead at them to go away. Some of them did go back a yard or two, and then they stood staring at Bob Pretty, wot come up as bold as brass and knocked at the door.

"Wot's this I 'ear?" he ses, when Henery Walker opened it. "You don't mean to tell me that the pore old gentleman has really gone? I told 'im wot would happen if 'e came to lodge with you."

"You be off," ses Henery Walker; "he hasn't left you anything."

"I know that," ses Bob Pretty, shaking his 'ead. "You're welcome to it, Henery. if there is anything. I never bore any malice to you for taking of 'im away from us. I could see you'd took a fancy to 'im from the fust. The way you pretended 'e was your great-uncle showed me that."

"Wot are you talking about?" ses Henery Walker. "He was my great-uncle!"

"Have it your own way, Henery," ses Bob Pretty; "on'y, if you asked me, I should say that he was my wife's grandfather."

"Your—wife's—grandfather?" ses Henery Walker, in a choking voice.

He stood staring at 'im, stupid-like, for a minute or two, but he couldn't get out another word. In a flash 'e saw 'ow he'd been done, and how Bob Pretty 'ad been deceiving 'im all along, and the idea that he 'ad arf ruined himself keeping Mrs. Pretty's grandfather for 'em pretty near sent 'im out of his mind.

"But how is it 'is name was Josiah Walker, same as Henery's great-uncle?" ses Bill Chambers, who 'ad been crowding round with the others. "Tell me that!"

"He 'ad a fancy for it," ses Bob Pretty, "and being a 'armless amusement we let him 'ave his own way. I told Henery Walker over and over ag'in that it wasn't his uncle, but he wouldn't believe me. I've got witnesses to it. Wot did you say, Henery?"

Henery Walker drew 'imself up as tall as he could and stared at him. Twice he opened 'is mouth to speak but couldn't, and then he made a odd sort o' choking noise in his throat, and slammed the door in Bob Pretty's face.

IN THE LIBRARY

The fire had burnt low in the library, for the night was wet and warm. It was now little more than a grey shell, and looked desolate. Trayton Burleigh, still hot, rose from his armchair, and turning out one of the gas-jets, took a cigar from a box on a side-table and resumed his seat again.

The apartment, which was on the third floor at the back of the house, was a combination of library, study, and smoke-room, and was the daily despair of the old housekeeper who, with the assistance of one servant, managed the house. It was a bachelor establishment, and had been left to Trayton Burleigh and James Fletcher by a distant connection of both men some ten years before.

Trayton Burleigh sat back in his chair watching the smoke of his cigar through half-closed eyes. Occasionally he opened them a little wider and glanced round the comfortable, well-furnished room, or stared with a cold gleam of hatred at Fletcher as he sat sucking stolidly at his brier pipe. It was a comfortable room and a valuable house, half of which belonged to Trayton Burleigh; and yet he was to leave it in the morning and become a rogue and a wanderer over the face of the earth. James Fletcher had said so. James Fletcher, with the pipe still between his teeth and speaking from one corner of his mouth only, had pronounced his sentence.

"It hasn't occurred to you, I suppose," said Burleigh, speaking suddenly, "that I might refuse your terms."

"No," said Fletcher, simply.

Burleigh took a great mouthful of smoke and let it roll slowly out.

"I am to go out and leave you in possession?" he continued. "You will stay here sole proprietor of the house; you will stay at the office sole owner and representative of the firm? You are a good hand at a deal, James Fletcher."

"I am an honest man," said Fletcher, "and to raise sufficient money to make your defalcations good will not by any means leave me the gainer, as you very well know."

"There is no necessity to borrow," began Burleigh, eagerly. "We can pay the interest easily, and in course of time make the principal good without a soul being the wiser."

"That you suggested before," said Fletcher, "and my answer is the same. I will be no man's confederate in dishonesty; I will raise every penny at all costs, and save the name of the firm—and yours with it—but I will never have you darken the office again, or sit in this house after to-night."

"You won't," cried Burleigh, starting up in a frenzy of rage.

"I won't," said Fletcher. "You can choose the alternative: disgrace and penal servitude. Don't stand over me; you won't frighten me, I can assure you. Sit down."

"You have arranged so many things in your kindness," said Burleigh, slowly, resuming his seat again, "have you arranged how I am to live?"

"You have two strong hands, and health," replied Fletcher. "I will give you the two hundred pounds I mentioned, and after that you must look out for yourself. You can take it now."

He took a leather case from his breast pocket, and drew out a roll of notes. Burleigh, watching him calmly, stretched out his hand and took them from the table. Then he gave way to a sudden access of rage, and crumpling them in his hand, threw them into a corner of the room. Fletcher smoked on.

"Mrs. Marl is out?" said Burleigh, suddenly.

Fletcher nodded.

"She will be away the night," he said, slowly; "and Jane too; they have gone together somewhere, but they will be back at half-past eight in the morning."

"You are going to let me have one more breakfast in the old place, then," said Burleigh. "Half-past eight, half-past—"

He rose from his chair again. This time Fletcher took his pipe from his mouth and watched him closely. Burleigh stooped, and picking up the notes, placed them in his pocket.

"If I am to be turned adrift, it shall not be to leave you here," he said, in a thick voice.

He crossed over and shut the door; as he turned back Fletcher rose from his chair and stood confronting him. Burleigh put his hand to the wall, and drawing a small Japanese sword from its sheath of carved ivory, stepped slowly toward him.

"I give you one chance, Fletcher," he said, grimly. "You are a man of your word. Hush this up and let things be as they were before, and you are safe."

"Put that down," said Fletcher, sharply.

"By —, I mean what I say!" cried the other.

"I mean what I said!" answered Fletcher.

He looked round at the last moment for a weapon, then he turned suddenly at a sharp sudden pain, and saw Burleigh's clenched fist nearly touching his breast-bone. The hand came away from his breast again, and something with it. It went a long way off. Trayton Burleigh suddenly went to a great distance and the room darkened. It got quite dark, and Fletcher, with an attempt to raise his hands, let them fall to his side instead, and fell in a heap to the floor.

He was so still that Burleigh could hardly realize that it was all over, and stood stupidly waiting for him to rise again. Then he took out his handkerchief as though to wipe the sword, and thinking better of it, put it back into his pocket again, and threw the weapon on to the floor.

The body of Fletcher lay where it had fallen, the white face turned up to the gas. In life he had been a commonplace-looking man, not to say vulgar; now Burleigh, with a feeling of nausea, drew back toward the door, until the body was hidden by the table, and relieved from the sight, he could think more clearly. He looked down carefully and examined his clothes and his boots. Then he crossed the room again, and with his face averted, turned out the gas. Something seemed to stir in the darkness, and with a faint cry he blundered toward the door before he had realized that it was the clock. It struck twelve.

He stood at the head of the stairs trying to recover himself; trying to think. The gas on the landing below, the stairs and the furniture, all looked so prosaic and familiar that he could not realize what had occurred. He walked slowly down and turned the light out. The darkness of the upper part of the house was now almost appalling, and in a sudden panic he ran down stairs into the lighted hall, and snatching a hat from the stand, went to the door and walked down to the gate.

Except for one window the neighbouring houses were in darkness, and the lamps shone tip a silent street. There was a little rain in the air, and the muddy road was full of pebbles. He stood at the gate trying to screw up his courage to enter the house again. Then he noticed a figure coming slowly up the road and keeping close to the palings.

The full realization of what he had done broke in upon him when he found himself turning to fly from the approach of the constable. The wet cape glistening in the lamplight, the slow, heavy step, made him tremble. Suppose the thing upstairs was not quite dead and should cry out? Suppose the constable should think it strange for him to be standing there and follow him in? He assumed a careless attitude, which did not feel careless, and as the man passed bade him good-night, and made a remark as to the weather.

Ere the sound of the other's footsteps had gone quite out of hearing, he turned and entered the house again before the sense of companionship should have quite departed. The first flight of stairs was lighted by the gas in the hall, and he went up slowly. Then he struck a match and went up steadily, past the library door, and with firm fingers turned on the gas in his bedroom and lit it. He opened the window a little way, and sitting down on his bed, tried to think.

He had got eight hours. Eight hours and two hundred pounds in small notes. He opened his safe and took out all the loose cash it contained, and walking about the room, gathered up and placed in his pockets such articles of jewellery as he possessed.

The first horror had now to some extent passed, and was succeeded by the fear of death.

With this fear on him he sat down again and tried to think out the first moves in that game of skill of which his life was the stake. He had often read of people of hasty temper, evading the police for a time, and eventually falling into their hands for lack of the most elementary common sense. He had heard it said that they always made some stupid blunder, left behind them some damning clue. He took his revolver from a drawer and saw that it was loaded. If the worst came to the worst, he would die quickly.

Eight hours' start; two hundred odd pounds. He would take lodgings at first in some populous district, and let the hair on his face grow. When the hue-and-cry had ceased, he would go abroad and start life again. He would go out of a night and post letters to himself, or better still, postcards, which his landlady would read. Postcards from cheery friends, from a sister, from a brother. During the day he would stay in and write, as became a man who described himself as a journalist.

Or suppose he went to the sea? Who would look for him in flannels, bathing and boating with ordinary happy mortals? He sat and pondered. One might mean life, and the other death. Which?

His face burned as he thought of the responsibility of the choice. So many people went to the sea at that time of year that he would surely pass unnoticed. But at the sea one might meet acquaintances. He got up and nervously paced the room again. It was not so simple, now that it meant so much, as he had thought.

The sharp little clock on the mantel-piece rang out "one," followed immediately by the deeper note of that in the library. He thought of the clock, it seemed the only live thing in that room, and shuddered. He wondered whether the thing lying by the far side of the table heard it. He wondered—

He started and held his breath with fear. Somewhere down stairs a board creaked loudly, then another. He went to the door, and opening it a little way, but without looking out, listened. The house was so still that he could hear the ticking of the old clock in the kitchen below. He opened the door a little wider and peeped out. As he did so there was a sudden sharp outcry on the stairs, and he drew back into the room and stood trembling before he had quite realized that the noise had been made by the cat. The cry was unmistakable; but what had disturbed it?

There was silence again, and he drew near the door once more. He became certain that something was moving stealthily on the stairs. He heard the boards creak again, and once the rails of the balustrade rattled. The silence and suspense were frightful. Suppose that the something which had been Fletcher waited for him in the darkness outside?

He fought his fears down, and opening the door, determined to see what was beyond. The light from his room streamed out on to the landing, and he peered about fearfully. Was it fancy, or did the door of Fletcher's room opposite close as he looked? Was it fancy, or did the handle of the door really turn?

In perfect silence, and watching the door as he moved, to see that nothing came out and followed him, he proceeded slowly down the dark stairs. Then his jaw fell, and he turned sick and faint again. The library door, which he distinctly remembered closing, and which, moreover, he had seen was closed when he went up stairs to his room, now stood open some four or five inches. He fancied that there was a rustling inside, but his brain refused to be certain. Then plainly and unmistakably he heard a chair pushed against the wall.

He crept to the door, hoping to pass it before the thing inside became aware of his presence. Something crept stealthily about the room. With a sudden impulse he caught the handle of the door, and, closing it violently, turned the key in the lock, and ran madly down the stairs.

A fearful cry sounded from the room, and a heavy hand beat upon the panels of the door. The house rang with the blows, but above them sounded the loud hoarse cries of human fear. Burleigh, half-way down to the hall, stopped with his hand on the balustrade and listened. The beating ceased, and a man's voice cried out loudly for God's sake to let him out.

At once Burleigh saw what had happened and what it might mean for him. He had left the hall door open after his visit to the front, and some wandering bird of the night had entered the house. No need for him to go now. No need to hide either from the hangman's rope or the felon's cell. The fool above had saved him. He turned and ran up stairs again just as the prisoner in his furious efforts to escape wrenched the handle from the door.

"Who's there?" he cried, loudly.

"Let me out!" cried a frantic voice. "For God's sake, open the door! There's something here."

"Stay where you are!" shouted Burleigh, sternly. "Stay where you are! If you come out, I'll shoot you like a dog!"

The only response was a smashing blow on the lock of the door. Burleigh raised his pistol, and aiming at the height of a man's chest, fired through the panel.

The report and the crashing of the wood made one noise, succeeded by an unearthly stillness, then the noise of a window hastily opened. Burleigh fled hastily down the stairs, and flinging wide the hall door, shouted loudly for assistance.

It happened that a sergeant and the constable on the beat had just met in the road. They came toward the house at a run. Burleigh, with incoherent explanations, ran up stairs before them, and halted outside the library door. The prisoner was still inside, still trying to demolish the lock of the sturdy oaken door. Burleigh tried to turn the key, but the lock was too damaged to admit of its moving. The sergeant drew back, and, shoulder foremost, hurled himself at the door and burst it open.

He stumbled into the room, followed by the constable, and two shafts of light from the lanterns at their belts danced round the room. A man lurking behind the door made a dash for it, and the next instant the three men were locked together.

Burleigh, standing in the doorway, looked on coldly, reserving himself for the scene which was to follow. Except for the stumbling of the men and the sharp catch of the prisoner's breath, there was no noise. A helmet fell off and bounced and rolled along the floor. The men fell; there was a sobbing snarl and a sharp click. A tall figure rose from the floor; the other, on his knees, still held the man down. The standing figure felt in his pocket, and, striking a match, lit the gas.

The light fell on the flushed face and fair beard of the sergeant. He was bare-headed, and his hair dishevelled. Burleigh entered the room and gazed eagerly at the half-insensible man on the floor-a short, thick-set fellow with a white, dirty face and a black moustache. His lip was cut and bled down his neck. Burleigh glanced furtively at the table. The cloth had come off in the struggle, and was now in the place where he had left Fletcher.

"Hot work, sir," said the sergeant, with a smile. "It's fortunate we were handy."

The prisoner raised a heavy head and looked up with unmistakable terror in his eyes.

"All right, sir," he said, trembling, as the constable increased the pressure of his knee. "I 'ain't been in the house ten minutes altogether. By —, I've not."

The sergeant regarded him curiously.

"It don't signify," he said, slowly; "ten minutes or ten seconds won't make any difference."

The man shook and began to whimper.

"It was 'ere when I come," he said, eagerly; "take that down, sir. I've only just come, and it was 'ere when I come. I tried to get away then, but I was locked in."

"What was?" demanded the sergeant.

"That," he said, desperately.

The sergeant, following the direction of the terror-stricken black eyes, stooped by the table. Then, with a sharp exclamation, he dragged away the cloth. Burleigh, with a sharp cry of horror, reeled back against the wall.

"All right, sir," said the sergeant, catching him; "all right. Turn your head away."

He pushed him into a chair, and crossing the room, poured out a glass of whiskey and brought it to him. The glass rattled against his teeth, but he drank it greedily, and then groaned faintly. The sergeant waited patiently. There was no hurry.

"Who is it, sir?" he asked at length.

"My friend—Fletcher," said Burleigh, with an effort. "We lived together." He turned to the prisoner.

"You damned villain!"

"He was dead when I come in the room, gentlemen," said the prisoner, strenuously. "He was on the floor dead, and when I see 'im, I tried to get out. S' 'elp me he was. You heard me call out, sir. I shouldn't ha' called out if I'd killed him."

"All right," said the sergeant, gruffly; "you'd better hold your tongue, you know."

"You keep quiet," urged the constable.

The sergeant knelt down and raised the dead man's head.

"I 'ad nothing to do with it," repeated the man on the floor. "I 'ad nothing to do with it. I never thought of such a thing. I've only been in the place ten minutes; put that down, sir."

The sergeant groped with his left hand, and picking up the Japanese sword, held it at him.

"I've never seen it before," said the prisoner, struggling.

"It used to hang on the wall," said Burleigh. "He must have snatched it down. It was on the wall when I left Fletcher a little while ago."

"How long?" inquired the sergeant.

"Perhaps an hour, perhaps half an hour," was the reply. "I went to my bedroom."

The man on the floor twisted his head and regarded him narrowly.

"You done it!" he cried, fiercely. "You done it, and you want me to swing for it."

"That 'll do," said the indignant constable.

The sergeant let his burden gently to the floor again.

"You hold your tongue, you devil!" he said, menacingly.

He crossed to the table and poured a little spirit into a glass and took it in his hand. Then he put it down again and crossed to Burleigh.

"Feeling better, sir?" he asked.

The other nodded faintly.

"You won't want this thing anymore," said the sergeant.

He pointed to the pistol which the other still held, and taking it from him gently, put it into his pocket.

"You've hurt your wrist, sir," he said, anxiously.

Burleigh raised one hand sharply, and then the other.

"This one, I think," said the sergeant. "I saw it just now."

He took the other's wrists in his hand, and suddenly holding them in the grip of a vice, whipped out something from his pocket—something hard and cold, which snapped suddenly on Burleigh's wrists, and held them fast.

"That's right," said the sergeant; "keep quiet."

The constable turned round in amaze; Burleigh sprang toward him furiously.

"Take these things off!" he choked. "Have you gone mad? Take them off!"

"All in good time," said the sergeant.

"Take them off!" cried Burleigh again.

For answer the sergeant took him in a powerful grip, and staring steadily at his white face and gleaming eyes, forced him to the other end of the room and pushed him into a chair.

"Collins," he said, sharply.

"Sir?" said the astonished subordinate.

"Run to the doctor at the corner hard as you can run!" said the other. "This man is not dead!"

As the man left the room the sergeant took up the glass of spirits he had poured out, and kneeling down by Fletcher again, raised his head and tried to pour a little down his throat. Burleigh, sitting in his corner, watched like one in a trance. He saw the constable return with the breathless surgeon, saw the three men bending over Fletcher, and then saw the eyes of the dying man open and the lips of the dying man move. He was conscious that the sergeant made some notes in a pocket-book, and that all three men eyed him closely. The sergeant stepped toward him and placed his hand on his shoulder, and obedient to the touch, he arose and went with him out into the night.

W.W. Jacobs – A Short Biography

William Wymark Jacobs was born on September 8, 1863 in the Wapping district of London, England. An author, humorist and dramatist, Jacobs is best remembered for the enduring classic tale of horror - "The Monkey's Paw".

As a youth, Jacobs grew up near the Wapping docks in London, where his father was a wharf manager. The family's first home was home was a house on a River Thames wharf.

The docklands setting would show up frequently in his later literary output. Jacobs, the wharf rat, and his three siblings lost their mother when they were all still young children. Their father, William Gage Jacobs, remarried and fathered a further seven children with his erstwhile housekeeper Ellen Florey. Although he grew up surrounded by poverty, Jacobs himself received a formal education in

London, first at a private prep school and later at the Birkbeck Literary and Scientific Institute (now part of the University of London and known as Birkbeck College).

Jacobs' adult working life began with a clerical position at the Post Office Savings Bank. The job was not a stimulating one but Jacobs put his imagination to good use and started to write short stories, sketches and articles, many of which appeared in the Post Office house publication "Blackfriars Magazine."

Although Jacobs did receive his fair share of rejection slips at the beginning of his career, many works written during this period of clerical employment appeared in the "Idler" and "Today" magazines, both of which were edited by noted humorist Jerome K. Jerome, who had taken a liking to Jacobs' stories.

From 1898, Jacobs also published stories in "The Strand", a popular, monthly fiction and general interest magazine. The arrangement stayed in place for most of his life and many of the works in Jacobs' subsequent collections – including the nautical serialization A Master of Craft (1899-1900) - appeared there first.

Jacobs' first volume of collected works was published in 1896. Many Cargoes, a selection of sea-faring yarns, established Jacobs as a popular writer and humorist with a penchant for authentic dialogue and trick endings (critics of the day referred to him as the "O. Henry of the Waterfront").

A year later he published a novelette, The Skipper's Wooing, and in 1898 and another collection of short stories titled Sea Urchins. These works painted vivid, if imaginatively stretched, pictures of dockland and seafaring London with colourful characters (such as "The Night Watchman", Ginger Dick) that now seem archetypal.

Many of Jacobs' periodical publications and first editions were illustrated with woodcuts and ink drawings, as was still the custom at the turn of the 20th century. The author worked regularly with artists such as E.W. Kemble, who had illustrated Mark Twain's Adventures of Huckleberry Finn and Harriet Beecher Stowe's Uncle Tom's Cabin, and his good friend Will Owen, who eventually became a household name on the strength of his iconic Bisto Kids, Bovril and Lux Soap advertising posters.

By 1899, Jacobs was able to quit the post office and finally begin a career making a living as a full-time writer.

He married the noted suffragist Agnes Eleanor Williams (who had been jailed for her protest activities) in 1900. They set up a household in Loughton, Essex as well as living part of the year in central London. The couple went on to have five children together though their marriage was considered an unhappy one.

The publication of two short novels: At Sunwich Port (a romantic tale of rival sea captains in the fictional seaside community of Sunwich standing in for the actual East England community of Sandwich, Kent) and Dialstone Lane (another small town romance involving intrigue and buried treasure), in 1902 and 1904 respectively, cemented Jacobs' reputation as one of the leading British authors of the new century.

On the foundations of a continuing ability to write for his audience he was readily published though he never strayed too far from what was becoming his familiar, dependable style. There followed a string of further successful publications, including Captain's All (1905), Night Watches (1914), The

Castaways (1916), and Sea Whispers (1926). Jacobs published eighteen books in all during his lifetime; thirteen collections and five novels.

As a storyteller, Jacobs is perhaps better remembered for a handful of brief tales of the supernatural than for his popular nautical-themed works. The most famous of these, The Monkey's Paw, originally appeared as part of the 1902 short story collection The Lady of the Barge. It is an economically written story about a shriveled talisman, a monkey's paw that brings grief and horror in the wake of all too literal wish granting. The story has been adapted for other media repeatedly, starting with a one-act play performed at London's Haymarket Theatre in 1903. There have been multiple film adaptations of the story in the modern era; some of us are familiar with its appearance in an episode of the popular animated series, The Simpsons.

Another macabre gem, The Toll-House, was published as part of the collection Sailor's Knots in 1909. Jacob's once again employs a sparse style to tell the story of a group of men who spend the night in a famously haunted house on a dare (a noticeably similar narrative concept was put to use in the much earlier play The Ghost of Jerry Bundler, which had launched Jacobs' parallel career as a dramatist back in 1899 when it was produced at the St. James Theatre in London). Innovative at the time of writing, these sparingly written, atmospheric ghost stories are now familiar classics of the supernatural genre.

Though prolific in his younger years, Jacobs' productivity dropped dramatically after the start of World War I. Yet even in self-imposed semi-retirement Jacobs was still recognized as a leading humorist, ranked alongside such writers as P. G. Wodehouse and George Birmingham. He enjoyed continuing influence and elevated status among his fellow writers as evidenced by these comments attributed to his colleague Henry James:

"Mr. Jacobs, I envy you. You are popular! Your admirable work is appreciated by a wide circle of readers; it has achieved popularity. Mine never goes into a second edition."

James' literary fortunes would, of course, change, but his back-handedly complimentary admiration is compelling evidence of Jacobs' reputation as a writer and humourist both for his audience and his perhaps more admired literary colleagues.

Though Jacobs would create little in the way of new work after 1911, he was still writing. In these later years, seemingly burnt out creatively, Jacobs concentrated more on writing dramatizations and adaptations of his existing stories, including Beauty and the Barge (a film version starring Margaret Rutherford was also released in 1937) and In the Dark (a one act play that is often performed pr published with The Monkey's Paw adaptation).

Though admired by loyal readers throughout his lifetime, Jacobs has been almost completely forgotten since. Critics are at a loss to name a single reason why - Jacobs is universally considered to be a fine and imaginative literary craftsman. But, as critic John Wain suggested in a 1960 essay, perhaps Jacobs' humour may have been too gentle to persist into the cruel and sarcastic modern era, his dry pokes at proletariat hardship no longer suiting the times.

Nonetheless, Jacobs' legacy remains solid: he continued Dickens' (a writer with whom he is also often compared) tradition for sharing working class stories in authentic vernacular. And polished narratives such as The Monkey's Paw set a standard for the clever use of horror in fiction and popular culture that endures to this day. Indeed recently his works have begun to show an increased demand and appreciation in a world that is constantly looking over its shoulder.

William Wymark Jacobs died in a North London nursing home in Hornsey Lane, Islington on September 1st, 1943, just a week before his 80th birthday.

W.W. Jacobs – A Concise Bibliography

NOVELS AND SHORT STORY COLLECTIONS
MANY CARGOES (SHORT STORIES) (1896)
THE SKIPPER'S WOOING (1897)
SEA URCHINS (SHORT STORIES) (1898) aka MORE CARGOES
A MASTER OF CRAFT (1900)
LIGHT FREIGHTS (SHORT STORIES) (1901)
THE LADY OF THE BARGE (SHORT STORIES) (1902)
AT SUNWICH PORT (1902)
DIALSTONE LANE (1902)
SALTHAVEN (1908)
CAPTAINS ALL (SHORT STORIES) (1911)
NIGHT WATCHERS (SHORT STORIES) (1914)
DEEP WATERS (SHORT STORIES) (1919)

SHORT STORIES (INCLUDING THOSE USED IN THE COLLECTIONS ABOVE)
A BENEFIT PERFORMANCE
A BLACK AFFAIR
A CASE OF DESERTION
A CHANGE OF TREATMENT
A CIRCULAR TOUR
A DISCIPLINARIAN
A DISTANT RELATIVE
A GARDEN PLOT
A GOLDEN VENTURE
A HARBOUR OF REFUGE
A LOVE KNOT
A LOVE PASSAGE
A MARKED MAN
A MIXED PROPOSAL
A RASH EXPERIMENT
A SAFETY MATCH
A SPIRIT OF AVARICE
A TIGER'S SKIN
ADMIRAL PETERS
AFTER THE INQUEST
ALF'S DREAM
AN ADULTERATION ACT
AN ELABORATE ELOPEMENT
AN INTERVENTION
AN ODD FREAK
ANGELS' VISITS
BACK TO BACK
BEDRIDDEN

TWO OF A TRADE
THE UNDERSTUDY
THE UNKNOWN
THE VIGIL
WATCH-DOGS
THE WEAKER VESSEL
THE WELL
THE WHITE CAT

THE GHOST OF JERRY BUNDLER (1899) (In London)

A MASTER OF CRAFT (1922)
THE MONKEY'S PAW (1933)
OUR RELATIONS, a Laurel & Hardy film, "suggested by" to Jacobs' "The Money Box." (1936)
FOOTSTEPS IN THE FOG, from the short story The Interruption. (1955)